Shell Shock:
the diary of Tommy Atkins

Edited by Neil Blower

FireStep
Press

www.firesteppublishing.com

Firestep Press
an imprint of Firestep Publishing

FireStep Publishing
13 Hunloke Avenue
Eastbourne
East Sussex
BN22 8UL

www.firesteppublishing.com

First published in this format by FireStep Press

ISBN 978-1-908487-02-5

Cover design FireStep Publishing
Typeset by Liz Jones
Printed and bound in Great Britain

Dedications

This book is respectfully dedicated
to all past, present and (sadly) future
members of HM Armed forces and all
those who have given their lives in the
service of this country.

For Sammi and Ethan,
you are my world.

Acknowlegements

My thanks to Ryan Gearing and everyone at FireStep for taking a chance and publishing this work; all staff and students at the University of Salford, especially Ursula Hurley, David Hamilton, Ben Mapp and Daniel Lamb for their support; the living legend that is Steve Griffiths; and all at Combat Stress including Sue Garnett, Michelle O'Brien; all the guys and girls of the Manchester group, Neil and Stephen in communications; Hussien Al Alak for all his support in promoting the book; Jenny Laing for her helpful editorial guidance; and finally my family and friends.

Contents

Foreword

Shell Shock: the Diary of Tommy Atkins is an important book because it addresses a very modern problem and it is both the first offering of a new writer and an important part of his road back to normality. I say back to normal because he was diagnosed with Post Traumatic Stress Disorder (PTSD) after his service with the Army in Iraq and for those suffering from PTSD their reality is not normal and not a place they want to be.

PTSD affects all walks of life, but for those who have developed the condition as a result of their service for the Crown, we all owe a care. Modern times have brought turbulence that is confusing, alarming and astonishing all in one; the modern wars that stemmed from 9/11 and their consequences rumble on ten years later. The Credit Crisis coupled with a now gone profligate government and crazy socialist experiments with the education system of the nation have left a generation with no apparent hope or focus and an apparent indifference to discipline and yet no one to blame. The pursuit of faux celebrity has replaced duty and national pride and the understanding of the vital link between having things and working hard for them has been lost.

But from the ranks of the young have come – from all walks of life and including many who have chosen to make the UK their home – an admirable group of young men and women who have dared to serve and volunteered for HM Forces. These young tigers from the same streets and towns so decried for their indiscipline have generated a force of such standing, discipline and excellence that they are the envy of the world. The impact of their service and example will be one of the touchstones of our age when we come to look back.

But it comes at a price. Many have given their lives and many others have suffered life-changing injuries in pursuit of our collective goals. But it is the unseen scars that worry most. It is the damage that cannot be seen and which is often disguised or denied by these who suffer and need help. This is PTSD.

Shell Shock: the Diary of Tommy Atkins is a glimpse into that world of confusion, doubt and dislocation. It is of course a fiction, but perhaps for the young man next to you on the train or on the football terrace a reality.

If we ever forget that they went to war on our behalf – regardless if you agree with the politics or not, as the young men and women of HM Forces share the same lever you have over those decisions in the form of the ballot box, except the consequences for them are more than a subject for discussion over a croissant – then we fail them.

Their salvation and lifeline from the black hole of PTSD is our collective awareness and willingness to help. If we resolve to be patient, understand and help we can defeat the plaque for PTSD that threatens amongst the best of us all.

Colonel Tim Collins, August 2011

Introduction

Oh, but it's Tommy this and Tommy that,
and 'Chuck him out, the brute!'
But it's 'saviour of his country'
when the guns begin to shoot.

Rudyard Kipling

When, my old friend Tommy Atkins sent me his diary
with a view to getting it published I was a little bit
taken aback. I hadn't seen Tommy since we did Basic
training together. He told me his story and that he had
Post Traumatic Stress Disorder (PTSD). He wanted
me to turn his diary into a readable book.

I'm a mature student doing a degree in English
literature. I am by no means an editor.

The book you are holding is the culmination of a
long process, by Tommy and me.

Tommy Atkins served six years in the army and
did a tour of Iraq and two tours of Afghanistan; he
was present when three of his comrades lost their
lives and on his return was diagnosed with PTSD and
advised to keep a diary to help him cope.

When I first received the diary it was, well, a
mess. He didn't write every day and he only kept a
record of the months instead of individual days – all I
have done is put it in a logical order.

Tommy would be the first to admit that his handwriting is not neat. So I persevered with it and as I deciphered the content I began to see something. I recognised what Tommy was saying and could relate to it: the anger, the sleepless nights, etc.

Tommy's story is heartbreaking but also very honest and very brave.

The bookshops are packed to the rafters with row upon row of books about war: fiction and non-fiction. This book is not about war. It's about what happens when soldiers leave the army and return home from one.

In the armed forces, Post Traumatic Stress Disorder is something of a taboo. No one talks about it, but it is there nonetheless.

Post Traumatic Stress is a normal reaction to an abnormal situation. It can affect people in different ways, to greater or lesser degrees. For Tommy, the effect was profound since he suffered from most, if not all the symptoms.
(A list of signs and symptoms can be found on page 17 , but for more detailed information go to www. combatstress.org.uk)
PTSD is nothing to be ashamed of – but tell that to a squaddie!

My role in this has been simple; I typed up the diary and corrected Tommy's spelling (if you are expecting beautiful prose, then you are holding the wrong book) and changed his language where appropriate.

I make no apologies for Tommy's vocabulary: he was after all a twenty-three-year-old British soldier and the reality is, squaddies swear a lot.

I hope you enjoy reading it as much as I enjoyed putting it together and hopefully you will gain at least some understanding of what surviving a war and living with PTSD is like.

Thank you.

Neil Blower
Spring 2011

Signs and Symptoms of Post Traumatic Stress Disorder

Below is a list of some of the most common symptoms of PTSD:

- Anger – getting heated very easily and at things other people might consider trivial
- Nightmares
- Flashbacks – re-living the traumatic event/ events
- Feelings of guilt
- Depression
- Abuse of alcohol/ drugs/ food
- Difficulty falling and staying asleep
- Difficulty making new friends and new relationships
- Avoidance of places and people.

For more information on this and the number of people it affects, please visit the website of Combat Stress - www.combatstress.org.uk

Shell Shock:
the diary of Tommy Atkins

JANUARY

Dear Diary,

Well, Doctor Harper says that writing a diary might help with the nightmares. I've never done this before. It's a bit weird, talking to no one. He says I can put down whatever I want: my thoughts and feelings. He told me to try and keep it as clean as possible. "Fat chance", I told him and he just laughed. Anyway, here goes.

Today is my last day in the army and I've been busy packing up my room and messing about trying to find everyone who needs to sign my papers. I'm all done now though and I'm sat here in this empty room, my telly and all my stuff is in the car ready to go. So I thought I might as well do this.

It feels very weird. It's all over now. I'm moving on. It no way feels like six years. Jesus, I was just a kid when I joined. I'd barely left school, then I went into the Careers Office and signed up, did my training, joined the unit and a couple of months later I was in the desert.

Anyway, gotta go now, a few of the lads want to buy me a pint before I leave. So, see you later.

Dear Diary,

I left the army today. It feels great. Driving out of those gates for the last time, then driving back home. Freedom, Baby. I listened to that Michael Bublé song, *Feeling Good*, about ten times. For the first time in a long time, I feel happy. When I got home the house was empty, Mum and

Dad were still at work so I unpacked some of my stuff and, you know what? My bedroom hasn't changed much since I left; I mean, I must have slept in here about a hundred times when I was home on leave but I always had to go back, now I don't.

I can't wait to see Shell later. I'm gonna pick her up from work. God, I've missed her, now I'll never have to leave her again. I love that girl more than she will ever know. She stood by me and I'm grateful for that. She's gorgeous and I still don't get why she's with me. All the letters and parcels she sent when I was on operations cheered me right up. It made it all worth it. What's the point in fighting when you have nothing to come home to?

Anyway gonna go now, I might put a DVD on.

Dear Diary,

It's half two in the morning and I can't sleep. I don't know why. Shell's upstairs, I picked her up from work. My God, the traffic was a nightmare. I know they call it rush hour, but Jesus, no one can drive any more, people darting everywhere, pulling out without indicating, driving up each other's arses. If I get a job in town, I'm taking the train.

When we got back to mine, Mum and Dad were already home, not talking as usual. They need to get that shit sorted whatever it is. We had tea, Mum did spag bol. Then we all watched Big Brother, my Mum and Shell are really into it, I never saw the point of it, people sitting in a house, watching people sitting in a house. Shell says it's good 'cos this is the celebrity version, but I didn't know any of them.

Anyway, then we went to bed and we made love, well actually, to be honest we went at it like rabbits. I could get used to being home every night.

22

Dear Diary,

I'm absolutely knackered. I didn't get to bed until gone four. I've just got back from dropping Shell off at work. She needs her own car, I can't be doing this everyday it's a nightmare. Forty-five minutes for a ten-minute journey any other time, but at 8'o clock? *No!*

The whole world wants to get into town then. It's funny seeing all the people trying to get to work, it must do their heads in knowing they have to do it all again at the end of the day.

I suppose that will be me soon though, joining the rat race.

Dear Diary,

Sorry I haven't wrote in a couple of days, I've just been really busy. I've applied for a few jobs the resettlement guy sent me, but to be honest they all seem really crap, so I think I might apply for the police or the fire brigade.

With my experience and training I should have no problem. The fitness wouldn't be too hard and I've already got the background checks and security clearance.

I saw the news before, it broke my heart. Two more lads came home through Wootton Bassett, poor bastards. It's the families that get to me the most, I'll never forget when Kev went and his Mum asked me what happened 'cos she knew I was with him at the end. What could I say to her? I couldn't even look her in the eye: "Sorry Mrs Cartwright, but your little boy was too fucked up from being blown to bits to say any meaningful last words and I was too busy trying to put him back together". I just wanna cry for them and then when they ask shit like, "Do you think it's worth it, Tommy, the war? Are we doing good out there? Tell me he didn't die for nothing".

I remember in Basic when we got let out for our first weekend and Kev kicked off with some students for spilling that girl's drink, the lunatic. I miss that twat.

Dear Diary,

I've done nothing today. It's been well boring; all I've done is watch DVDs. I thought about going for a run, but couldn't be arsed. I might join a gym when I start work. That will be weird, doing PT on my own, although no dickhead PTI shouting and screaming at me is gonna be nice.

I think I'm goin soft. I watched *'Love Actually'* before and I cried my bloody eyes out. I'm glad no one was about.

Dear Diary,

In a really good mood today. Me and Shell went for a drink with Ian. The big poof's not changed a bit; he's still playing the field trying to find Mr Right, the slag. I use to call him my civvy best mate, now I suppose he is my only best mate.

It only seems like two minutes ago when he came out and you wouldn't believe his Dad's reaction! I still don't get what all the fuss was about, crying 'cos your son's gay. So what, he fancies men? He's still your son; he was still my mate, that didn't change just because he likes cock.

The prick cheered me up with all the letters he sent detailing his adventures in gay land, the dirty bastard sucked off a taxi driver once 'cos he didn't have any money.

Christ, if a bird did that there would be uproar, but we just laughed it off with Ian.

He thinks I should go for the fire brigade: wonder why? He said he didn't like skinny blokes like me even if I were a fireman. Cheeky git.

Dear Diary,

Can't be arsed.

Dear Diary,

Sod the fire brigade, stupid bastards. It's a joke. I rang the recruitment line today and basically I'm not fucking good enough to be a fireman.

The guy on the phone asked me a few questions. I told him about the army and my experience and you know what he said?

"Sorry lad but you're not the type of person we require."
WHAT!

He said that they were only taking on women and gay or black men at the moment, because they had a certain number of each to give positions to: government regulations, apparently. Bullshit. So it's all right to call in the army when the bastards go on strike, when there's no one else around to save people's lives, but we're no good to do it full time. Wankers.

Sod them. I'll apply for the coppers, everyone's always whinging that there's not enough of them, anyway.

Dear Diary,

I don't know what's up with Mum and Dad. They are either always fighting or they don't speak at all. I asked my Dad what was the matter and he just said, "When you've been married as long as we have, you have your ups and downs." And that was it. I wonder if it's 'cos this year they've been married twenty-five years. Bloody hell, that's a long time. I hope me and Shell can last that long. Maybe if my Dad didn't work late most nights and go away every other weekend playing golf, then my Mum might not be so pissed off all the time, moody bitch.

Dear Diary,

I sent my application for the police off today. It took me ages 'cos my handwriting's shit. I used a ruler to write with so it would be neat and didn't use joined up so it would be readable. They wanted to know everything. I left the box for qualifications blank 'cos what could I put – couple of NVQs from the army?

Anyway, I went to the post office 'cos I want to send it Next Day Delivery and when I got there the queue was out the door; twenty bloody minutes just to send a letter. The place was full of foreigners, it was like downtown Kabul, and all the doleys were all in there getting their beer tokens, the tramps. I felt like saying to one of the mutants, "What's the point of you? What are you about? Bloody oxygen thief".

And then to top it all we had today's knobhead. Why is it that every day, wherever you go, there's always a world-class knobhead – the guy behind the counter who served me – miserable bastard. I just want to send a letter: 'Service with a Smile' would be nice and some eye contact, you pathetic, ignorant prick.

Five pound fifty to send a letter Next Day Delivery! I could have driven there and given it them myself for less than that. Dick Turpins, all of them! At least *he* wore a mask.

Anyway, when I finally got out of there I hadn't eaten in days so I went to Gregg's for my dinner – steak slices and sausage rolls – then I went home.

I'm really tired today; I had another nightmare last night and it was well screwed up. I was in this future war against robots, but it was like World War Two with the uniforms and weapons we had, I was running into a firefight and then it all went in slow motion and I could see the bullets coming towards me like on the *Matrix*. I got hit; then I woke up.

Dear Diary,

Bored again today, I watched *Lord of the Rings*: well good films, them. Love the big battle scenes and the banter between the dwarf and the elf. Funny shit.

Picked Shell up from work and we went out for tea. We went to this American-style place, I had a massive steak with BBQ sauce and melted cheese and Shell had chicken. It was really nice.

What's with people these days? Nobody has any manners – it's disgusting. There was this prick at the table next to us who started clicking his finger at the waitress and then spoke to her like she was a piece of shit, I could have knocked him out, the poor girl was only doing her job and it was mad busy. Saying please and thank you costs nowt and it's the same everywhere you go. It's not hard, is it?

"Can I have, whatever, please?" and when you get it, "Thank you" or "Thanks" or "Cheers".

That was today's knobhead.

When we got back to mine, my Dad was still at work, as usual and my Mum was already on her second bottle. We just went upstairs and watched the telly.

Dear Diary,

Done nothing today. After I dropped Shell at work I came home. My Dad had left his paper and I read this article about a little lad whose Dad had been killed over there. I cried. It was so sad, this little boy, he was only eight years old, his Dad was his hero and now he'll never see him again; it said that he let off a load of balloons at the funeral.

Don't know words to say what I feel, just want to keep repeating all the filthiest I know in a long stream but it makes my hand ache: fuck, shit, cunt, balls, pillock, bastard, the whole lot, but it doesn't help.

I wonder how the Sarge's daughters are getting on. They will be at High School now. I can't imagine it, growing up without a Dad, it's heartbreaking.

I couldn't read any more after that, so I watched the telly, *This Morning* was on and they were showing how to bake a wedding cake, then what the latest fashions were. God it was boring.

Then I heard this noise from outside, a really loud banging and scraping, I went to the window and a big lorry drove off. Our next door neighbour Betty had been delivered a new washer.

The idiots just left it outside. How out of order. I went out to give her a lift, how the hell can an 80-year-old woman get a washing machine in her house. The poor woman was really struggling.

So, I got it inside; Christ, it was heavy but I managed to get it into her kitchen. She was so grateful. She tried to give me a fiver for my trouble but I said it was OK.

I asked her if she needed any help setting it up, but she just said, "No Tommy you've done enough, I'll be all right." She was looking at the instructions and clearly didn't have a clue. So I said, "Here, let me take a look."

It was total gobbledegook, but I did it in the end.

Afterwards she made me a brew and gave me a scone. In her living room I noticed a picture of her husband when he was young, in uniform somewhere.

"Thank you for this, Tommy, you're a good boy. My husband would have liked you, being a fellow soldier. He was in Korea," she said.

Bloody hell, I thought. Korea: that was a real war.

She said that everyone was very proud of me and that she really felt for my Mum and Dad when I was away.

"Your Dad didn't sleep," she said. "He would stay up all night watching the news. He told me once that every time he heard a car on the street his heart would sink thinking it was an officer and a chaplain."

Anyway, I went back home and I couldn't stop thinking about what she said. I've never really thought about how my Mum and Dad and Shell felt when I was on operations, it must have been agony, not knowing from one day to the next. Least I knew where I was and what I was doing. What did I put them through? It was my choice, not theirs, and yet they suffered because of me.

I feel like shit.

Dear Diary,

This is bullshit. I got a letter today telling me I'm not good enough to be a copper.

Not good enough to be a copper?

NOT GOOD ENOUGH?

"Sorry Mr Atkins but you're just not suitable for the police".

Wankers.

Not enough qualifications, my arse!

What has knowing about Shakespeare got to do with catching villains? A lot of paperwork involved, is there? What do they do? Sit there all day writing fucking *War and Peace?* No wonder the country's gone to shit and the crime rate's through the roof; the police are too busy debating philosophy. Cunts.

I was good enough to fight the Taliban but not criminals. Bullshit, bullshit, bullshit. I would be a bloody good copper. How hard can it be to spot a scumbag? You know when someone's up to no good, you can spot it a mile off. They want to try doing it when the sods don't even speak English.

My Dad fell out with me 'cos I hit the roof.

He said, "Calm down, what did you expect, you have no qualifications and no experience?"

I just told him to fuck off back to work.

Shell said not to worry about it and I'll find something else.

"What?" I asked, "I don't want to be a drone, with a bullshit job that does nothing, I want to do something that matters, that's productive."

She said that there's not a lot of jobs or employers who value ex-squaddies, so I said, "Fine, I'll go back to the bloody army, if that's all I'm good for."

She told me to grow up.

Dear Diary,

Today's been shit. I've apologised to Shell. I don't know why I was so angry, but anyway I decided to go to the Job Centre and see what they've got. I need to start work soon 'cos I'm absolutely skint.

So when I got to the Job Centre, you can't just speak

to an advisor, oh no. You have to use these machines and search for a job yourself, unless you're a tramp and then they'll speak to you, 'cos that's all it was in there: tramps and slobs.

Have a wash, you dirty bastards.

Jesus.

So I finally found one that looked good and didn't ask for any qualifications. It's for an engineering firm who do chrome plating – a polisher's job, whatever that is. Anyway, I gave them a ring and I have an interview tomorrow. So, hopefully, if it goes well I could start next week. I'm quite excited really, a proper job, it's quite cool. Maybe I could join the Union, or go on strike.

Dear Diary,

Absolutely buzzing. I've got the job and as of next week I'll officially be Tommy Atkins, metal polisher. I'm over the moon.

The interview went really well, the guy seemed to be well impressed, he liked the fact that I'd been in the army and had discipline and was punctual. It's not something I ever thought about; being on time is just a natural thing. If you have to be somewhere at ten o'clock, you're there at least ten minutes early. It's not hard, is it, turning up for work or an appointment on time? The way he was talking, was as if it was this big problem. Anyway I'm chuffed to bits and we are going out to celebrate.

Dear Diary,

It's half one in the morning and I can't sleep, again. I had a really bad one tonight, I don't even remember what it was about, I just woke up screaming and I was covered in sweat and I mean drenched. I wish they would go away. For fuck's sake, it was ages ago since I got back. What the hell is wrong with me? Soldiers aren't supposed to feel like this. I might see if I can ring Colonel Harper and ask him for some advice.

FEBRUARY

Dear Diary,

I know it's been a while but I just haven't had the time to write. I started my new job a couple of days ago. It's goin' OK so far. I have to be in at 08:00 every morning and I finish at 16:30, so it's not bad. I'm what's called a polisher, which means I have to wear a Noddy suit most of the day 'cos of the fumes or whatever. It can be hard but mostly its mind numbing. We get a ten-minute break in the morning for a brew and a fag, then half an hour for dinner and then another ten-minute break in the afternoon. It's like being at school, they have a bell that goes off to signal when it's time for a break, then it goes off again when you should be back at your post.

The guys I work with are all a lot older than me. There's a couple my age, but I don't really like them much, they're a bit, I don't know, empty.

Every time I talk to them I just think to myself, "Shut up, you knob, what do you know?"

I mean, all anyone seems to talk about is football, or whinging about the managers and money. I like football, I like playing it and watching it and going to a match when I can, but, Jesus Christ, change the record. These guys live and die by the Saturday results and woe betide anyone if their team loses, you'd think someone had raped their wives.

Anyway, so I just keep to myself and get on with it. We are there to do a job. The money's shit, it's only minimum wage, which drives these bastards crazy. The way they talk you'd think that they had been really screwed over. They all think they should be on fifty grand a year or something. For what? Chrome-plating a bit of metal? Or polishing it?

It makes me laugh. None of them would last two

minutes in Basic.

Anyway, I phoned Colonel Harper. I never know whether to call him Sir or Doc. I asked him about my nightmares and he said I need to see my GP 'cos I'm not in the army any more, I'm not their responsibility, it's down to the NHS.

I'm not gonna see the doctors over this. It's only some nightmares. I can live with them, and I don't want to go on tablets. I don't need them; I'm not some pathetic mental midget who can't cope.

Dear Diary,

Got paid today. It's shit: three hundred and fifty quid after tax and shit. I've worked my bollocks off. Seven hundred quid a month. I can't be doin' with this getting paid every two weeks, all my Direct Debits are set up for monthly.

I was gonna ask Shell to get our own place. I've been looking at stuff for rent and you can't get a cardboard box for less than £500 a month. If we moved in together we would be skint all the time, I asked my Dad to work out what it would cost with bills and everything. I pretty much need to earn double what I'm getting now to even think about going out and buying clothes and shit. It pisses me off, all her friends' boyfriends have mint jobs and they go out all the time and buy them presents and go on flash holidays and here's me, can't even afford to take her out to bloody McDonalds.

I wouldn't blame her if she left me for someone else: what the hell have I got going for me? She said that when I was away she told everyone how proud she was of me and that I was a hero.

Her *hero*.

Some hero I turned out to be, I couldn't save my best

friend; I couldn't save anyone, not the Sarge, not Johno, not even that little girl. A hero? Heroes don't have nightmares and they don't earn minimum wage.

Anyway, I can't be bothered any more, I'm gonna watch *Doctor Who* on DVD. I might get a takeaway.

Dear Diary,

When I got home from work today, my Dad, the fruit loop had only gone out and bought a Wii, the mad idiot. Someone told him that you can play golf on it and that it would improve his game. Oh My God, I was hurting from laughing. He took it proper seriously, and my Mum just sat there and said nothing. I thought I was gonna piss.

He looked like a drunken duck the way he waggled his arse about. Then he let Shell have a go and she only went and beat his score, didn't she?

His face was priceless. So then he had another go. And this is the point when I lost it completely. He took a swing and lost his balance and fell back on his arse. The idiot couldn't even get up – he was like a beached whale. I told my Mum to ring Greenpeace. He told me to fuck off.

Dear Diary,

It's 04:30 and I've been up all night. We went to bed about eleven; me and Shell had a bit and then went to sleep. Well, she did. I couldn't get to sleep 'cos of the noise, I thought someone was breaking in; I've been on pins all night.

Still, if I don't sleep, at least I won't have any nightmares.

Dear Diary,

I rang in sick today, I really couldn't be arsed with work. I've just laid about all day, read the paper, watched a bit of telly. What's with it, with these mongs on Jeremy Kyle? Christ, I thought I was messed up, but these guys were just, well, just unreal.

What planet do they live on? I mean, not one of them could talk properly; they looked like refugees from the planet Knobhead, in the inbred Fecknut Galaxy. Jesus. And these are the people I risked my life for?

No wonder all the politicians are on the fiddle! If I had to represent those sub-human, missing-link half-wits, I would jump on that gravy train and ride it to the end of the line. The prime minister should make a list of everyone who's ever been on that show and send them out to find IEDs [Ed: improvised explosive device]: the robots the engineers use have a higher IQ than these twats.

So, after that, I gave up on the shit that was on telly and watched another bit of *Doctor Who*. It's good, I never watched it before, I just thought it was for kids. Billie Piper would get it all over the place; not too keen on Katherine Tate as the assistant though.

So, after the Doctor had saved the day again, I got a text off Shell asking me if I wanted to meet her and a few of her work-mates for a drink. That's where I'm off to now, so if I'm not too pissed later I might write again.

Dear Diary,

Never, ever, doing that again. My God, I could have slapped every one of the jumped up bastards.

So I go to meet her, and things don't start off very well 'cos the barman pissed me off.

"No, I don't want a bottle, you prick, I want it in a pint

glass."

What kind of bar doesn't do pints?

So I got a Jack and Coke. Oh, sorry, they only do Pepsi. Thank you for that, knob jockey. And then to top it all, diet or ordinary.

"Do I look like I'm on a diet, dickhead? Just give me a drink."

God.

So then I meet her friends, who I thought would all be women, but no, there was a few guys from her office, all there in shirts and ties.

They all looked at me like I had two heads, not just them but everyone in there seemed to be staring at me.

Anyway, the conversation quickly turned to the army.

"So how long were you in?"

"What did you do?"

"My auntie's cousin's son is in the army, do you know him?"

WHAT? Listen luv, there are one hundred thousand people in the British army, and yes, I know every one of them. Moron.

And then this knobhead from the IT department pipes up later on, *"So how many people have you killed?"*

At this point I lost it, so I just said, "Including women and children or just the Taliban?"

His face dropped: the prick.

So of course I'm bad bastard then. Shell was livid. Fuck her and fuck her friends and fuck fucking Nick, the smarmy knob, with his suit and fucking hair-do, the greasy cunt. He was all over Shell, the scumbag.

And you know what, on the way home she fuckng defended the bastard.

"Oh we are just good friends.

"Bollocks," I said. "He well wants to get in your knickers."

"No he doesn't," she said.

So I said, "Listen, men and women can't be friends, at least not from a man's point of view. The only time a man's nice to a girl is if he fancies her."

Christ, she hit the roof: started shouting and

screaming at me. I couldn't be arsed, so I told her to go get a tampon.

She called me a sexist bastard, so I asked her if there were any fat girls in the office.

She said there were a couple, so I asked if Nick or any of the other blokes were friends with them as well. She didn't say a single word. Ha!

It's true, I know what men are like, the only way a man and a woman can be friends and just friends, is if the man's gay. If a straight guy is friends with a girl then he either wants to bang her or at least would do if given the opportunity. Fact of life.

Dear Diary,

I don't want to go to hell, but that's where I'm going. It doesn't matter what religion is right; I've taken human life and every religion says that that is a sin.

I've killed more people than Jack the Ripper. It was my job: my duty. But I'm still a killer. Are there people out there who miss their son or their brother or Dad, because of me?

I still see their faces, every one of them.

I've thought about going to see a priest about it, but what is he going to say? *"Oh it's OK, the Bible says killing is a sin, but for you, Tommy, the Almighty is willing to make an exception."*

I know I'm supposed to think that it was them or me, and, well, what if it was their family who had to bury them? But I can't stop thinking about them.

Then I think of Kev and his Mum's face, and I want to burn every one of the dirty (Ed: illegible). I want to hurt them, punish them.

And then the faces come back.

God, I want to forget everything. I want everything to

be like it was before. I wish I could just regenerate into someone else and forget all about Tommy Atkins.

I'm sleeping on the couch 'cos Shell has fallen out with me. I can't sleep. I've had quite a bit to drink and the room is spinning.

What the hell is it all about?

Dear Diary,

I made Shell breakfast in bed to apologise. I told her I was sorry. She said she wants me to go and see a shrink. I said I'd think about it, but I've already done that.

Then we had the make-up sex, oh yes.

She's in the shower, then we are going to the shopping centre, I might get some new CDs and the next series of *Doctor Who*.

Dear Diary,

Just got back from shopping. The entire world was there. Could we find a parking space? Could we, hell.

Why these knobs in 4x4s have to park over two spaces, is beyond me, selfish pricks, I was gonna leave a note on one of their windscreens saying 'Learn to fucking drive, cunt!', but Shell stopped me.

Jesus, it was busy. You couldn't move, people pushing and shoving everywhere. And what is it with these pillocks who walk in front of you and then stop to look in a window, so you nearly bang into them?

I do not like crowds, it does my nut. Get out of my personal space, dickhead.

Why do people in a queue have to stand right up your arse? Do I smell nice?

Do you want to bum me, knobhead? No? Well get away from me, I do not want to feel your rancid breath on the back of my head.

There was this one guy who even followed me to the till; right at my shoulder he was. I could feel him stood behind me, so when I'd been served I turned round and banged right into him and nearly knocked him on his arse. "Oh, sorry, mate, didn't see you there."

Trying to put your dick in me, were you?

Shell fell out with me, said I was being an old man and should cheer up, it was fun. Fun! What is fun about being shoved around and being shoulder to shoulder with strangers all day? What's fun about spending most of your time in a queue waiting to be served?

Christ!

And why do women think that men find it interesting to stand in a girl's clothes shop like some pervert while they try on a hundred different things? No, it drives us mad. We don't give a monkey's if the dress is nice or not or if the shoes match or the bag. I think she looks nice in anything. She would look sexy if she wore a bin bag, but no, I have to stand there and nod my head like a muppet.

And then to top it all, it took forty-five minutes to get out of the car park, because of course, everyone had to leave at the same time.

So anyway, it wasn't a total wash-out: I got some new DVDs. Shell wanted me to get some new clothes but I couldn't be arsed.

Ian texted me to see if we wanted to go out, but I just couldn't be bothered, so we got a takeaway and watched telly.

Dear Diary,

I'm in a really good mood. Everyone else is still in bed. I slept really well, like a baby, I feel so fresh. I woke up and turned over and there she was: Shell. She looked so beautiful, so peaceful. I love her so much, I can't even find the right words to describe how she makes me feel, I would do anything for her, I want to spend the rest of my life with her. One day I want to have kids with her.

I think I'm gonna take her away for Valentine's Day. We could go away to a hotel in the country. I don't know where I'm gonna get the money from though; I wonder how much that will cost.

Dear Diary,

I phoned in sick again today. I just can't be arsed with being stood there all day. It's so boring.

So I've been looking on the internet for a hotel to take Shell to for Valentine's Day. There's some really nice ones, but My God, they are expensive. I might see if my Dad can lend us some money.

Dear Diary,

Stayed off again today. My Dad said I'm gonna get sacked. I don't give a shit, though. I think I'm gonna look for something else. Minimum wage, ha! I could spit.

Read the paper today. Was it shit, or was it shit?

It was shit.

Why do I want to know if some slapper has split up

with her boyfriend? How the hell is that front page news? A child dies every three seconds in Africa, apparently. The country's in the shit, we're still at war, the planet is dying and the press in their infinite wisdom decide: "Oh yeah, I know what people want to read about, other people's pointless existence."

Maybe if people spent more time worrying about their own lives the world might not be such a shithole.

Sometimes I just feel so alone. I know I've got Shell and my Mum and Dad, but I just feel like I'm the only person who gives a shit, the only one who sees that the world is one fucked-up place. All anyone seems to care about is money, or the football, or celebrities. I'm sick to death of pointless conversations about nothing, bloody gossip and nonsense. I love Shell to bits but, why do I care if Becky from HR is shagging the boss or if the coffee machine broke or there was a fire alarm. I didn't write to her every time we had a contact. I didn't call and say, "Ooh, guess what? I went for a ride in a Chinook, today."

I just want a decent conversation with someone who's got half a brain; someone who's seen the world and travelled to more than just Ibiza.

No one has a clue how people in other countries live: we whinge if the bins don't get emptied. I'd love to see how people coped if we got invaded. If the power went off and there was no running water, Bloody hell, half these imbeciles would top themselves if they couldn't have their mobile: "Agh, my phone won't work, I can't text anyone". Oh, the horror! Pricks.

I'm just really fed up and I don't know why. I might go and get the car cleaned before I pick Shell up.

Dear Diary,

Absolutely buzzin'. My Dad said he would lend me the money to take Shell away. Get in. I'm gonna book it later. He said that I had to sort myself out and stop messing work about. He said that if I don't want to work there I should just quit and find something else before they sack me.

I can't wait to see Shell's face, it's gonna be mint.

Dear Diary,

Went into work today, it was OK. I told some of the lads about my Valentine's Day trip and one of them said he would get me some Viagra.

I said, "Cheeky bastard, what do I need Viagra for?" and he said "Trust me, you take half and she takes half, and then see what happens."

So I've asked him to get me some.

When I told Shell about the hotel she was chuffed to bits, I showed her the website, it does look really flash. We both got a bit giddy and had a bit right there.

Dear Diary,

Had a right laugh at work today, I got the Viagra; he gave me six pills for a fiver. He said make sure you only take half or you'll have a hard-on for days.

When I got home my Mum was well pissed off 'cos my Dad had to go away on business for a few days, so I said, "So what, he works hard and has an important job."
She just told me that I was too young to understand and

finished her wine while she made tea. Can't wait till we go away, Shell said she's gonna get some stuff from *Victoria's Secret*, oh yes.

Dear Diary,

It's been a few days, so here goes. The weekend away was absolutely brilliant. We had a really good time and the best sex ever. We talked a lot as well, about our future and things.

We set off on Saturday, traffic wasn't that busy. My Dad said he would let me borrow his Satnav, but I told him I didn't need it.

"Christ I said, I've found more remote places."

So I printed the directions off the internet so Shell could navigate.

The journey wasn't that bad, apart from the knobhead in the Audi. The prick got right up my arse; *want to see what's in the boot?*

Fucking idiot. I wouldn't mind, but I was in the slow lane doing 80 mph. *Oh, sorry, is 80 miles an hour too fucking slow?* That's what the other lanes are for dickhead. Dangerous bastards, why drive up peoples arse? There is no need for it at all – he would be the first one to complain if his kids were killed by some cunt driving too fast.

So, anyway, this cretinous sod was doing my head in, so I hit the brakes. And then . . . then the spunk bucket had the nerve to beep his horn at me. Cheeky bastard. Shell went mad, said what was I playing at. Then the idiot overtook, so I followed the wanker and got up his arse for a bit.

I wouldn't mind but he didn't do over 85 mph: the way he drove you'd think he would be off like a shot but no, obviously he didn't know he had a 3-litre engine or he was just a pussy.

Anyway so we got to the hotel and, my God, it was nice. Very modern and posh. The people there were very nice; they even carried our bags up to our room.

How much do you tip people? I've seen them do it on films but how much do they get? So I give the guy a fiver.

So then we chilled out and got ready for dinner, I raided the mini-bar and flicked through the TV channels. I started to watch the news; same old shit, politics and sport and another poor bastard at Wootton Bassett. It made me feel pretty guilty. Here I was about to go to dinner with a beautiful girl and somewhere tonight another family would be in shreds.

I turned the channel over to one of the music channels. Then Shell came out of the bathroom. My God, she looked so beautiful, so sexy. I was dead proud to have her on my arm and watch all the heads in the place turn to look at her.

The food was fantastic, it was a Valentine's Day theme and for dessert they did these heart-shaped biscuit things with strawberries and cream and sauce.

After dinner we went to the bar and had a few drinks and a good chat, she told me she loved me so much and that she wanted to move in with me. I felt on top of the world.

So then we went back to our room and while Shell was getting dressed, I had one of the Viagras. I took a full one 'cos I think that if you're gonna do something, do it properly. I cut another in half so she could take some and then she came out and fuck me, I did not need any pill. Just one look at her in that outfit and I was as hard as an elephant's tusk. She took her half and then, well, we did it all night.

Wow!

What Viagra does to women is beyond me: she turned into a bloody porn star. It was ace, absolutely brilliant. Six times, oh yes.

Anyway, in the morning, there was a knock on the door, and I forgot that we ordered breakfast in our room. Shell wouldn't go, so there's me, answering the door with

Blackpool fucking tower underneath my towel, the guy just smiled, "Breakfast sir, do you want me to bring it in?"
"Do I, hell," I thought.
So I took the tray off him. Christ, I didn't have to use my hands, I could have just balanced the thing on my cock. It was aching like mad – it felt like I had been lifting weights with it.

The thing lasted until we got home, so I had to get out of the hotel and pay the bill with a bloody stonker: God, it was embarrassing, walking round with a Mars bar in my pocket.

And driving! Jesus. Never, ever drive with a hard-on. Shell offered to help me out but I had to concentrate on the road; you know it's bad when you say no to a BJ.

Dear Diary,

My Dad's a prick.
The first thing he said when he got back was, "Have you got my money?"
No, dickhead, I've not, it's been three days since you gave it to me and have I been paid yet? No.
Anyway, I'm gonna make an appointment with the doctor. I just can't sleep and when I do, I have nightmares. Shell seems to think I need anger management classes. Bugger that. If everyone stopped being knobheads then maybe I wouldn't get so angry.

MARCH

Dear Diary,

Got my P45 today. I've not been in for ages so the manager rang up and asked if I was planning on coming back.

I said, "No". Just like that.

Now I'm out of work. My Dad hit the roof, Shell was pretty pissed but said that she understood, she knew I wasn't happy there. But she asked about us moving in together. I need a new job.

Dear Diary,

Went to see the doctor today. What a surprise, he put me on tablets. Prozac and sleeping pills. Great.

When I rang for an appointment, I asked to see the doc as soon as possible and she told me there was nothing available until next Thursday. What . . . the . . . hell?

So now, in this country, if you want to see your doctor you have to be near death's door or as she put it, "Is it a medical emergency?"

If it was a bloody emergency then I would ring an ambulance and go to A&E, wouldn't I?

So I told her, yes, it was medically urgent, and she didn't even ask what was wrong. I could have walked in there with no head for all she knew.

So I go there and I've not been for years: what a joke. They're not wrong when they say the NHS is screwed. I saw a poster for some shit, flu probably, but I couldn't tell because it was in every language but English. Jesus.

And then there was this old man, some foreigner, he was kicking off 'cos his interpreter was late. If he can afford a sodding interpreter why doesn't he just go private? One of the officers did that when he was on leave, got paid about seventy-five quid an hour just to translate for people. I should have learned another language.

So then I finally get in to see him and told him about my problem with sleeping and the nightmares and about the army. He said I sounded depressed and the first thing he did was give me a sick note for two weeks. Great. He said he was gonna refer me to a shrink, but it could take six months or longer, and then he gave me a script for the pills.

And that was it. So I go to the chemist to get my pills and they had me for £7.50. Next time I'm gonna tick the box that says pensioner.

Dear Diary,

Bored, bored, bored.

Dear Diary,

I'm not a bad person, I'm really not. Why Shell can't see that is beyond me. She thinks I'm a nutter, just because I shouted at the telly. Just because I show some emotion at things doesn't make me a weirdo.

She said it wasn't normal and people don't behave like that.

So I said, "What people?" and she said, "Everyone". Well, sod her and sod everybody else. If caring about things makes you a bad person then I must be evil.

I lost my rag 'cos there was this thing on the News about some poor kid who had been abused. The things these fucking cunts did to that little boy . . . So I just said that they should be shot and things. Why is that so bad?

Why? *Why* would you harm an innocent little child and hurt them and stuff? It makes me want to cry and then I'm made out to be lunatic? If a dog bit a kid it would get put down – that's a dog who knows no better – but when a person does that it's so much worse, it's pure evil and the bastards need to be made to suffer.

"But, oh no," Shell says, "what about justice?"

JUSTICE! A warm room and SKY. Don't have to work, just hang about all day playing cards. *Justice?* Not gonna bring the kid back, is it, or deter anyone else from being an evil cunt. Justice!

Anyway so now I'm some freako sleeping on the couch. Next time, she's gonna sleep on the couch, it's my house.

I still can't sleep so I'm gonna have some of my Dad's whisky and see if that will do the trick.

Dear Diary,

I might be getting a new job. I was flicking through the jobs pages and found one that sounds good. It's for a corporate security officer, ex-forces preferred.

It's shift work but the money sounds decent. From what I can make out from the ad it's basically stagging on. Or more like guard duty on camp.

Anyway I phoned up and they gave me an interview, no forms or nothing, which was good. It's for a bank, but this didn't sound like the Halifax. She mentioned something about a hedge fund. What the hell is a hedge fund anyway? Sounds like a church appeal, 'save our hedges.'

So anyway my interview is next week. I need to get a new suit. I'm gonna have to ask my Dad for another loan.

Dear Diary,

I could punch my Dad sometimes. He said he would lend me the money but I had to pay back double. WHAT!? That's nice of you, Dad. He said, why should he lend me the money when I have no job. He said I was a cheeky git, asking to borrow money when I couldn't afford to pay it back.

"Live within your means," he said.

So I have to go for an interview in a bin bag then, Dad?

So he wants me to pay back double when I have it. I said he was an evil bastard, preying on my desperation. He just said, "Welcome to the real world."

Dear Diary,

Feel really down today, why is anyone's guess. Just really miserable. Gonna go out tomorrow and get my suit and some new shoes. I hope I get the job, it sounds really good.

There is just nothing, nothing I can be arsed doing. Shell said we should go to the pictures. So that's where we went. The best part about the film was the trailers at the start. There are some good films coming out this year. Still not sure about 3D, it works for some films but on some it makes no sense, and the robbing bastards charge you for the glasses even if you have your own, what a racket. It cost us thirty quid for the two us tonight, with popcorn and coke and stuff. It's daylight robbery, how people with kids go on is beyond me.

Anyway off to bed now, I've took some tablets to help me sleep, so I'll see how it goes.

Dear Diary,

What is the point? Why is it everywhere you go someone always manages to mess you about?

We went shopping today and got my new suit. Shell does my nut: I don't want to look like some poncey actor, I want to look smart. But to her looking smart and tidy is old-fashioned, what is old-fashioned about a plain black suit? She said I should try something funky, whatever that is.

So we agreed to disagree and I got my suit and some new shoes, I even got a new shirt and tie. If I have to pay back double anyway, I might as well get my money's worth.

I'm quite nervous about this interview; last one I had was a long time ago. I doubt very much they will give me a tenner if I get it.

I remember when I took the oath and they gave me the Queen's Shilling, I bought a pack of fags and a McDonald's with it. Very Richard Sharpe that. My Mum and Dad said I should have had it framed, what the hell for?

Anyway I'm gonna look on the internet and get some tips on being interviewed.

Dear Diary,

I really miss Kev today; I can't stop thinking about him. His anniversary's not till May, but he's just on my mind for some reason.

Why him and not me? It just does my head in. A few seconds either way and it would be him and not me writing in this bloody thing. Well the twat couldn't write anyway, illiterate bastard, so that one's out.

Why? Why did he have to die? What for? To defend the country? To defend freedom and keep us safe?
He died for nothing. *Nothing!* All of it: all the training, all the gear, all for nothing. Because some stranger says so.
Here you go guys, you're off to a country no one's ever heard of, or gives a flying fuck about, because there are terrorists there. Really?
Got ICBMs [Ed: inter-continental ballistic missile] have they? I would love to see the Taliban attack London or Birmingham from one of their caves. They would have a long walk wouldn't they?

Oh, we will build schools and roads. For what? So when we leave, the bastards have an infrastructure? So it will be easier for them to oppress the people? So it will be easier for them to pick on women and children.

And these idiots who talk about it like they are experts – it's easy to comment from the safety of a newspaper office or a TV studio. I'd love to see some of these turds in a firefight. They should send out every MP and make them do a tour, greedy (Ed: illegible), then maybe we would get some decent kit. Jesus.

I just miss Kev, I wish he was here to cheer me up and tell me not to worry about the interview. He was always good at that.

Dear Diary,

Why is nothing ever simple? I've been looking on the internet all day for interviewing tips and, my God, there are loads. Bloody hell. Do this, do that, make sure you have eye contact, be confident, don't be over-confident. It's amazing how anyone gets any job with all this shit, what happened to just "be yourself"?

Dear Diary,

I can't sleep, it's my interview tomorrow and I'm shitting it. I keep thinking of all the questions they could ask and the right answers I can give; I keep going over it in my head. God, I wish I could sleep. Shell said not to worry and that I'll be fine, but what if I'm not? What if I balls it up and don't get it? What will I do then?

Dear Diary,

What a day. Oh My God. Never want to go through that again.
So I get into town with plenty of time and try to find a car park near the place, which was a nightmare, the one ways are a joke, it took me twenty minutes to get back round to where I started.
So I finally park and get to the place. My God, it's flash. I give my name to the receptionist and she tells me to go the 5th floor. So when I get there, there is another reception, which turned out to be the bank's, only it's not really a bank, it's an investment bank. Anyway so I'm

waiting there watching the News channel on the TVs they had in the reception – really nice ones they were, 42-inch plasma or LCD, I couldn't tell.

So then this guy comes out and introduces himself. His name is Graham and he is the head of security for the bank. Apparently he was in special branch and spent some time in Northern Ireland.

So we go in his office and there are a man and a woman behind a desk, it was the managing director of the bank and the head of HR, I thought it was bit much, but they said it was standard procedure for a position like this, 'cos I would have access to sensitive areas.

They asked me loads of questions: what if this happened or that happened. What would I do and all that shit.

So I just told them the truth. I didn't lie and I was just myself. I couldn't tell how it went; they just said they would be in touch. I told them all about the army and stuff. They even wanted to know about Shell; don't get what my girlfriend has to do with it, but they evidently did.

So that was it, and then on the way out, Graham shook my hand and it was really weird, he looked me in the eye and said, "Thank you. Not enough people tell you that, I bet."

So I just said, "No."

The weirdo – and he's gonna be my boss, if I get the job.

So then I go back to the car and find that I've been robbed. £8.50 for three hours, the wankers.

Dear Diary,

I've not heard anything about the job. It's only been a few days though. My Dad said that I shouldn't get my hopes up, which caused my Mum to go ballistic; she kept saying he should be more supportive. Shell said I was in with a good chance from what I told her about the interview.

I hope I get it, the money's good: twenty grand a year. But what I like the most it that it's a proper job, in an office and I get to wear a suit, I have always looked smart in a suit. But hey, I've never really needed to wear one before, have I?

I don't know what I'm gonna do if I don't get it, there's just no jobs I could do, I don't have any qualities anyone's looking for.

Anyway gonna go now, me and my Dad are going to the driving range.

Dear Diary,

It's that time in the morning again. No nightmares this time 'cos I have not been to sleep yet.

What the *hell* does everyone keep staring at me for? Everywhere I go I catch people looking at me. Why? Have I got a cock hanging off my head?

And then I thought we were being followed home, this guy followed us all the way from the driving range, I was gonna carry on past ours and drive to the cop station.

My Dad said, "Don't be an idiot," but I was convinced. He even indicated at the same time as me. But then he turned off before we got to ours.

Anyway, I'm up now, so no one breaks in. I heard a noise in bed before and now I'm gonna stay up just in case.

Everyone thinks I'm being paranoid, but sod them, I know what I see and hear.

I'm gonna watch *Countdown* in a minute. I started to watch an old Bond film but I didn't like it so I turned the channel over. It's weird – I use to love James Bond. Anyway, see you later.

Dear Diary,

Chuffed to bits. I got a call before from Graham; I've got the job. Absolutely brilliant.

We're goin' out to celebrate, I'm just buzzin. My Mum and Dad are really pleased. Well, my Dad just wants his money back, but how cool.

I start next week; I have to go in before, to get my uniform, which is just a grey suit, with white shirt and red tie. The first week is an induction week where they brief me on all the stuff I need to know, Health and Safety and fire procedures. They're gonna go over the stuff they do as well and what my job will entail. Absolutely mint.

Now me and Shell can start looking for our own place, I can't wait. It will be ace, she will be the last thing I see before I go to sleep and the first thing I see when I wake up, I can't think of anything better. Now she only stays a few nights a week and I miss her like crazy. Mint.

Dear Diary,

I'm just about to go to bed, Shell's at her Dad's, but I rang her before and told her the good news. She was well chuffed.

I'm in such a good mood; I can't believe the way it's turned out. Finally life is going the way I want it to, and hopefully I can put my past behind me and look forward to the future.

I can't wait to move in with Shell. Maybe I could do gardening and DIY on a Sunday and we can have BBQs in summer and have everybody round. Oh, it's gonna be great.

Anyway, my tablets are starting to kick in so I'm off to bed.

I might not write any more, 'cos I don't think I'll need to now. I reckon I can cope on my own. So if I don't write again, it's been fun, diary.

See you soon, maybe.

Dear Diary,

Hello again. Ignore what I said before about not writing: four fucking hours I was asleep.

The tablets are useless. I knew I should not have started taking them. Another fucking nightmare, this one was about who knows what. I was being chased round an industrial estate by this car that had guys in it that were shooting at me. They got me in a dead end and then shot me to fucking bits. And I woke up. For fucks sake, what the hell is wrong with me?

I feel like shit. I have been watching the news. What is wrong with the human race; why can't we sort it out? The government does my head in, the knobs, how hard is it to run the fucking country? It's not as if it's new, it's been around for centuries, but no, these idiots have to go and balls things up.

Why?

Why piss people off so much? Why do they do things that people hate?

Wankers.

Anyway gonna go and read for bit. My Dad's got loads of books so I'm gonna read one of them.

APRIL

Dear Diary,

Well, it's been a while; let me fill you in on what's been happening. I've started my new job. It's really good, all the people are really nice and the offices are well smart.

I have to work twelve-hour shifts, I do three days, four nights then get three days off and then I do four days, three nights then four days off. My four days off are always a Thursday until Sunday, and my three days off are a Monday, Tuesday and Wednesday. So it works out I work two out of three weekends, one on days, one on nights and the third I get off. It took me a while to get my head round 'cos it's quite complicated but now I'm fine.

The money is good as well, it's £6.59 an hour, so with the amount of hours I work I get roughly nineteen and a half grand a year, depending on extra shifts and bank holidays.

There's three of us on the team but I only see them at the start or end of the shift 'cos there is only one of us on by day or night. The other guys are quite cool from what I've seen, Bob is a sixty-year-old former Marine and Jack has been doing security for years, I think he's about forty but I don't want to ask.

Graham is really cool as well, he always asks my opinion on stuff, which is quite nice and so far there's not really any knobheads.

There are loads and I mean loads of fit girls who work here, all quite young too. Most of them have just finished Uni, 'cos to work here doing the money stuff they like, you have to have a degree.

Anyway, the first week I had my induction and got my uniform. Bloody hell I've put on weight. Now I'm a 32-inch waist. That's the biggest I've ever been in my life.

So, on the induction it was a lot of the usual shit about Health and Safety, fire drills and stuff about data protection. But the stuff about the money markets was good, I never knew that if you split up all the money floating about on the stock market then every man woman and child on the planet would get ten grand. It's been really good; I mean you get to learn a lot just by going for a fag.

I never knew that companies used their profits to buy shares in other companies, how mad is that?

So I asked one of the guys and he said, "Yeah, they do." That is crazy! So Tesco use the money they make and buy shares in Asda, and Asda do the same. And then they make adverts saying that they are the cheapest. What for? Why not just have one big company and make it cheaper for everyone? But it doesn't work that way apparently, it's against the law, something about monopoly. I wanted to make a crack about not passing Go, but I thought it would be better to keep my mouth shut.

It's mad, all this financial stuff and capitalism. I think I might have to read up on it, Shell still has some of her books from Uni, so I might borrow them for when I'm on nights.

Dear Diary,

Just finished my first run of nights and now I'm off for three days. God, I'm tired. Don't know why though. On nights it's well boring. I get in at about 18:30 so the other guy can get off; it's good 'cos they do the same for me. Then, by about half seven, everyone's gone home and then it's just me until the other guy comes back in the morning. All I have to do is a patrol of the floors every two hours, it is supposed to take thirty minutes but you can do it in fifteen. On the patrol I have to take the temperature of the computer room, if it goes above a certain temperature

I have to ring the IT manager and Graham. I mean if anything at all goes wrong I just pick up the phone, it's dead easy.

When I have done the patrol I go out for a fag and then have a chat with the guys downstairs who look after the whole building, they work for a separate company, not the owners. It's mad how this one building has so many different firms involved in running it. I mean the bank rents the space and so do the other companies in here – one's a law firm I think.

Anyway, the owners don't actually run the building, they pay a separate company to do that. Then that company pays a security company to supply guards for downstairs, and then they get in another company to do the cleaning and yet another company to do the maintenance. It's mad. Why?

I'm sure it would be cheaper for the owners to run it themselves and employ people directly for security and cleaning and what not. They always say cut out the middleman, I just don't get it.

So once I've done the patrol I just sit there for two hours bored out of my mind. I read the paper which took me until the second patrol to read cover to cover. So next time I'm gonna bring in some books. I might save up for a laptop as well 'cos they have wireless which I can connect to for free.

Anyway gonna go get my head down.

Dear Diary,

Went for a run today, and am I out of shape! I only did four miles and I was knackered, I need to give up the fags.

This week, me and Shell are looking at places to rent: a couple of houses but mostly flats. I'm really excited. I hope we find one we both like.

My Mum and Dad are gonna take us out for a meal for my birthday to some posh place in town. I can't believe it – twenty-three! I feel like an old man. It doesn't seem like two minutes since I was leaving school, God, loads has happened since then.

Sometimes I think that the army was just a dream, it's a million miles from here and sometimes I can't get my head around the fact that I've been to war. It's madness. I look round and sometimes it's like it didn't even happen.

Anyway gonna have a shower before I pick Shell up.

Dear Diary,

Me and Shell have seen a house we really like; it's a two-bed semi on a nice quiet cul-de-sac. It's part furnished as well so we won't need to buy much. Chuffed to bits. The only problem is they want two months' rent up front for a deposit. I can't be asking my Dad again so Shell's gonna ask her Mum and Dad for the money until we get on our feet.

Wow, I feel really grown up, like a proper adult now, looking at houses and shit, paying bills and going doing the weekly shop, it will be ace.

Gonna go for a pint with Ian later, not seen him in ages. It will be nice to catch up.

Dear Diary,

Well it's been an interesting couple of days. Had a drink with Ian the other night, and he was well pleased for me and Shell. He says we should have a house warming if we get it. He said he'll invite some of his pals. I told him to piss off; I'm not having a bunch of screaming fairies running round the place pissed up. Why is it that gay men turn into animals when they have a drink? Ian's the same, the more he drinks the camper he gets, it's well weird.

Anyway, my birthday was really good, Shell got me some new DVDs and aftershave that she said smelled really sexy. I don't really like it though, but I only wear it for her, so hey-ho.

My Mum and Dad got me a laptop and an iPod. Chuffed to bits: I've wanted one for ages, and the laptop's made by Apple as well. It's got a wireless router so I can use it at work and I can watch DVDs on it, so no more being bored at work.

And then, when we went for the meal, afterwards, when we were having coffee my Dad said he would give us the money for the house. I couldn't believe it and Shell nearly cried, we were both so happy.

My Mum had a face on though – she didn't seem that happy. Anyway, we get the keys next week. Oh yes, can't wait.

Dear Diary,

I have to be up in two hours and I'm wide awake, I've had about three hours' sleep. I've been on the internet downloading songs for my iPod, all the new stuff is pretty shit so I've been getting old songs mostly, and then they recommend you stuff based on your downloads, so then before you know it you've spent a fortune on songs you have never even heard of or wanted anyway.

Gonna go sort my uniform out and polish my shoes before I have a shower, so see you later.

Dear Diary,

Been on days this week. It's OK, but I think I prefer nights when there's no one about. When I had my dinner the other day, I got chatting to the canteen manager when I went outside for a fag. He asked me how I was settling in and I said, "Fine, it's going well."
He asked about where I worked before so I told him about the army and stuff. He said his brother was over there at the minute with the Engineers. Anyway, he seemed like a nice guy.

So then I went to get some food and when I got to the till, he said that it was on the house and anything I wanted, just ask. What the fuck for I don't know, but I'm glad 'cos it's well expensive. He said he'd leave out some stuff for me when I'm on nights as well, but not to tell the other guys.

Anyway, so I'm having my dinner and someone had left a paper on the table which I was reading, then this knobhead walked past and said, "You know there's no Page Three in there, don't you mate."

I could have put him through the window. Arrogant bastard. And then he walked off laughing with his chums. Prick. For the life of me I don't know how I didn't leather him. But it's a good thing I didn't 'cos I would probably have got sacked.

Anyway, later on in the afternoon I had a good chat with Graham in his office. He told me some stories about Northern Ireland: it was bloody rough over there. It was before my time, but I didn't realise how many guys we lost. No one really talks about it any more, a few of the senior

NCOs in the regiment went but they never told us anything in detail.

So then Bob came in early and I went home. I start my nights tomorrow, so I'm off to bed early to try and get some sleep.

Dear Diary,

I feel well good today. I slept like a log. I didn't get up till gone one o'clock. I just chilled for a bit before I came into work. I'm on my own now, but I've got my laptop in my bag for later and Shell gave me a book to read. It's by this bloke called Karl Marx. She said I would find interesting 'cos of where I worked, but I don't understand a word of it.

Graham worked late and didn't go until about nine. He saw the book and laughed.

He said, "Don't let any of these see you reading that, they will go mad."

So I just said OK and then he left.

I don't get why he said that, it's only some guy from a hundred years ago writing nonsense.

Anyway, got to do a patrol now, so see you in a bit.

Dear Diary,

Karl Marx!!! What is the guy chatting on about. Confiscation of private property, my arse. Come round my house and try and take my shit and watch what happens to you, you dirty red bastard.

And this bollocks is what people learn at Uni? What a load of tosh. For someone who cared so much about the workers, I don't think he ever worked in a factory. Oh no.

Come back when you know what you're talking about, knobhead.

It pisses me off so much, it's the same today, people with money telling poor people how to live their lives and what's best for them. Er no . . . we can make up our own minds, thank you very much.

Communism worked for the Russians, didn't it? Oh yeah, and the Chinese. There's a billion happy fucking campers right there!

I don't want to be lectured at by some dickhead who's never done a day's work in his life. Went to Uni when he was seventeen, in the Victorian days. Yeah, he was working class wasn't he? Prick.

I hate hypocrites. These morons who want to save the planet and drive a hybrid or ride a bike everywhere! And what is wrong with these idiots who ride bikes? Fine, ride a bike but do you have to dress like a twat doing it, why, why are you wearing skin-tight lycra? Knob.

Are you on the Tour de France? No, you're in rush hour and it's pissing down.

And then the people who go to buy fair trade coffee and help out the farmers in Colombia to make themselves feel good and then at the weekend shove a bag of coke up their nose. Yeah, that will help stop the oppression of Third World farmers, won't it, cock jockey?

These pompous wind-bags who buy a hybrid and then go on holiday to the Seychelles, that's not far to go in a 7-4-7 is it? Oh, or did you go in a Zeppelin? So, well done you for doing your bit to help the planet.

It makes me so angry, all this bullshit. All the people who bang on about how bad the world is and how the Third World has a rough deal, well, join the Red Cross then. Don't come to me and bitch about the evils of the world. Get off your fat arse and go do something about it. No, you would rather whinge and moan and watch the X-Factor.

If it's one thing I learned from the army, it's that one man or woman can make a difference. Fact.

Dear Diary,

Just got in and I'm knackered, gonna go bed in a minute. I feel really down today. On the way home I just started crying: it's a good job no one was next to me at the lights. I don't know why, but I just started to get really sad and then I filled up and started to sob. What the hell is wrong with me, that can't be normal?

Anyway, see you later.

Dear Diary,

I'm in work again. Just finished a patrol. Ben the canteen manager has left me a load of stuff – sarnies and chocolate and a full pot of coffee and milk and sugar, I can't believe it. I hope he doesn't do it every night 'cos I will get really fat.

Me and Shell move into the house at the weekend, can't wait. We are gonna go to Ikea and get some stuff. Ian said he will help us move in and my Dad did as well. Not long now, buzzin'.

Dear Diary,

What a day. It's my last night tonight and I'm off tomorrow. I got up before and my Mum was crying her eyes out downstairs. My Dad the wanker has walked out, I couldn't believe it. After twenty-five bloody years he does one, and get on this, he's only been banging his secretary.

How original, Dad: an affair with your assistant. Prick. I could kill the bastard. And my Mum has known for months. What the hell?

All his stuff is gone, it's well mad; I can't get my head round it. My Mum is in absolute bits; I don't know what to do. What the hell can I do? I rang my Dad but he wouldn't answer, the coward, 'cos he knows I'll kick his arse. His secretary.

Jesus.

I always thought they were OK. But my Mum said that ever since I left for the army, something changed between them. She said when I left they had nothing else to talk about and their relationship just disappeared.

I feel like shit, I feel like it's my fault and if I hadn't joined the army then they might still be together, we might still be a family. My Mum said not to be stupid and it was nothing to do with me and that they both still loved me very much. It was always the three of us. What happens at Christmas now? What about the house?

My Mum said that they are gonna sell it – she can't live here any more, too many memories. Yeah, I know, all my memories, this is the house I grew up in, and now they are gonna sell it, Jesus.

That's why my Dad give us that money, the wanker, it was guilt money 'cos he knew he was gonna piss off. How low can you get, using money to wash away guilt and buying your child's affection! That's what a coward does. Real men don't do that. Be a Dad, be a man, talk to me and tell me everything will be all right, tell me you love me. Don't use your cash to replace your reasonability.

God, I'm so upset, I was gonna ring in sick but my Mum told me not to. I felt so bad leaving her on her own. When I told Shell, she cried. She said that my Mum and Dad always seemed really happy.

Just goes to show you never really know what goes on behind closed doors.

MAY

Dear Diary,

Ikea is shite. It must be the divorce capital of the world. My God, what a nightmare.

We went to get some new stuff for the house. I don't know why I bother 'cos what I say makes no difference what so ever.

"Do you like this, Tommy?"

So I say, "No, not really, let's get the other one," and what does she do? Gets the thing anyway. Why bother to even ask me, then? Jesus.

And Ikea must be like catnip for all the mutants and mongs that there are. I've never been anywhere that people are so stupid it makes you want to rip off your own arm and beat the shit out of them with it.

So you spend hours following the arrows like lemmings, so you have to go through a whole fake house. No, I want some glasses, I do not want a new kitchen or a mattress that they insist on showing how good it is by having a bloody glass case like some mattress museum. Why, *why*, do you have to walk round the whole place before you can get to what you want? Oh yeah, so you buy shit you don't need!

And then at the end of this epic fucking ordeal, what do they do? They try and placate you with 69p hot dogs and mini dime bars, crafty bastards.

And people fall for it. Me and Shell argued all the way round, then she has a hot dog and forgets everything.

"Oh, we should come back again, it's great, isn't it?"

Is it, hell? I won't be going back there. It's like a bad day in Basra.

So then, we get back home, and I wouldn't mind but we've only been in there a couple of days and what does she do?

"Tommy, I thought I asked you to do the pots?"

They're in bloody soak.

Jesus. What is wrong with not wanting to spend half an hour scrubbing last night's lasagne off an oven dish, when you can leave it in soak for a bit, and it just slides off? But, oh no, on Planet Shell where she's from, it is somehow unseemly and lazy and wrong to do that, because she wasn't brought up that way. In her house they did things properly.

Piss off. You and your perfect, judgmental, superiority complex. Look down your nose at everyone else's bloody family.

Why can we not have a dishwasher? Oh, because that's lazy.

LAZY!

It's the twenty-first century. Do we wash our clothes by hand? Do we, hell! We use a washing machine, so what is wrong with a dishwasher?

I tell you, I love her to bits but her family have messed her up good and proper, with some crazy, dyslexic work ethic and backward morals.

In Shell's family, it's OK to fuck over your brother and closest friends and cheat on your wife, and walk out on your kids. That's perfectly fine, but, not doing house work the right way? Well, bugger me, call in the Inquisition.

And then, then the cheeky bastards have the balls to judge me and say I'm not good enough for their Shell.

Not good enough!

I'm more of a man, a better person than all those small, petty-minded idiots put together.

Dear Diary,

Shell's upstairs in bed. What a night. It's funny how things turn out. We were having this blazing row about bloody housework and then the phone went.

It was Stacey, one of Shell's closest friends. I can't even find the words. Stacey's seven-year-old boy, Jamie.

Well, it turns out that, Jamie has cancer. *Cancer.*

He's seven years old. Seven. The poor little thing.

When I got back from Iraq he gave me a box of Cadbury's Heroes, 'cos he said I was his hero and when he grew up he wanted to be just like me. Bloody hell. And now, *now* the little kid who I use to play with when we visited might die. Just a little kid.

How's that right, how's that fair? If there is a God, he's got a sick sense of humour. What has Jamie ever done to anyone?

A sweet innocent little kid, whose Mum and Dad love him and would do anything for him. Seven years old. Why?

But that's the world we live in, isn't it. People who don't deserve the oxygen they breathe, get away with everything and horrible, vile people get health and happiness and a long life. And then children like Jamie get taken out before they have reached double figures. It's not fair. It's not right.

I can't help but think of Kev and Johno and the Sarge. They died for their country, it's tragic and it's heartbreaking. But they knew the risk, we all did. It was our choice to put our names on that dotted line. No one made us.

But Jamie, he hasn't signed up for anything; it's not his choice. Why? Why the fuck has this happened. A little boy who still believes in heroes. A little boy who believes that there are men in the world who right wrongs and fight the good fight. Bloody superheroes.

He reminds me of me when I was that age – into comics and cartoons. And now he has this horrible disease.

Is he in pain? Is he scared? As an adult I can't imagine

having cancer. But as a kid?

He said to me once, when I was on leave, "Uncle Tommy, are you a hero, do you save people and keep them safe?"

I lied. I told him I was. I told him that no one would hurt him as long as I was around and if anybody did then he should tell me.

The truth is heroes don't exist. And a man in a red cape and blue tights isn't gonna fly in and save the day. A man in a little blue box isn't going to make everything all right. Not even a superhero can cure cancer.

This world is fucking horrible: all that there is, is hate, and pain, and suffering.

I think I might ring my Dad. I haven't spoken to him in ages. Life's too short and no matter what's he's done, he's still my Dad.

Anyway gonna go try and get some sleep, we've got a big day tomorrow, we are gonna go and see Jamie in the hospital.

Dear Diary,

Not in the mood, I'll write again soon.

Dear Diary,

I don't know where to begin. Everyone is in absolute bits over Jamie. We went to the hospital to see him and it was horrible. A cancer ward is no place for anybody, let alone children. The whole place sent shivers down my spine, it felt like death. Stacey is in a mess, so is Karl,

Jamie's Dad.

What do you say to them? What can you say? *Oh it will be OK, he'll get better.* He goes in for chemo soon and then if that doesn't work they are gonna operate.

I just feel so helpless; all anyone can do is hope and wait.

All I can think about at the minute is the army, how weird is that? What's the point of it all? Everything we do, all the good we try to accomplish, all the stuff we want to do in our lives, means nothing 'cos at any time we can be struck down by this horrible disease.

And what's the point of war? It makes no difference whatsoever. People still die no matter how much you try and protect them. All that death, all that suffering. For nothing.

Anyway gonna go now, I have to tidy up before Shell comes home, or she'll have my life. Got to get your priority's right haven't you?

Dear Diary,

What is it with these call centres trying to sell you stuff. Good God, it's my day off, leave me alone. No, I do not want double-glazing; no, I'm not in debt; and no, I do want to claim for an accident. Jesus Christ. All day, and this is what people do for a living? Christ.

And then they're not content to just call you, oh no! Then they send some mutant round your house: "Hello Sir, who is your energy supplier?"
None of your business, that's who, now piss off."
But will they? Will they take no for an answer? Will they, balls?
This one guy, he didn't know when to leave it alone. Five times I told him we were not interested in changing our gas and electric supplier, but the prick insisted on showing me

a comparison on his knock-off ipad.

So I just said, "Listen mate, I've told you a few times that we are not interested, and besides, it's not you people who decide the prices it's the Russians and if they want to put up gas then they will and you idiots will have to charge accordingly. Now get off my property before I put your nose at the back of your head."

Then he just said, "No need for that, is there?"

"No mate, there's no need for you and your kind terrorising people in their own homes. Now fuck off."

These people need to go out and get real jobs.

Dear Diary,

I can't sleep. Again.

Dear Diary,

Me and Shell have had a right laugh today. It started this morning when we were in bed. We just talked about stuff for ages, then I let one rip and put her head under the duvet. God it was a bad one. So then we had a play fight which led to you know what.

Anyway then we got up and lazed about for a bit, then went down to the park and had a walk round. It was really romantic. We got ice cream; I've not had ice cream for ages, a '99' with a flake and strawberry sauce.

When we got back my Dad had left me message saying he wanted to meet up with us.

That's where we are off to now, to meet him and his new girlfriend, Lisa. Well actually she's his secretary, but whatever.

I'm in a really good mood, so sod it, live and let live.

Dear Diary,

We got a call from Stacey. Jamie's having an operation,
'cos the chemo didn't work like they wanted it to.

Oh yeah, and Lisa's not that bad. Don't get what my
Dad sees in her though, my Mum's well prettier. They want
to get married. Whatever. My Dad asked me to be his Best
Man. I told him I'd think about it. What's my Mum gonna
think? I hope she's not too upset.

Dear Diary,

Got home from work before and Shell hit the roof 'cos
I've not pegged the washing out.

What? Put it in the dryer for God's sake.

So before I could even tell her about my Mum, we were
having another row.

She says I've changed, and that I'm not the man I was.
"Oh, well, who am I then?"
She said she thinks I should see a shrink, so I said, "What
for?" and she just said I was a freak and should get my shit
together.

"What, because I can't sleep, because I actually show
some emotion at stuff?"
She said it's not normal to get as angry as I do.

She said she thinks I have post traumatic stress
disorder.

No. I had it. Now I don't. I had a few sessions with Doc
Harper before I left and now I'm fine. She said I wasn't fine

and that I need help.

Help with what? All the idiots in the world? Cos that's what I'm angry about. So then she came out with all this bullshit about manifestation, she says I have not faced up to what I've been through, which makes me get angry at stupid stuff and not be able to sleep.

So I just told her to fuck off. What did she know? She works in a nice safe office. And what does she know about traumatic experiences. Naff all.

Then she stormed out and went sulking upstairs.

And then, when I was banging about throwing the pots in the sink, I heard her sobbing from upstairs.

So I went up and she was lay face down on the bed, and my heart broke in two.

I gave a cuddle and told her everything would be all right, and I would try and change. I told her I loved her.

We made up and I told her about my Mum.

I called her on my dinner break and told her about my Dad and him getting married. She didn't say much, just "Oh, right."

Then she asked me what Lisa was like, so I told her she was a moose and that she was well more beautiful than her and that my Dad was a wanker.

So we are gonna go see her tomorrow, when I finish work.

Dear Diary,

Just got back from seeing my Mum. I'm really worried about her: she says she's fine but I don't believe her. I was making a brew and I saw loads of empty bottles in the bin.

The house is on the market and she's got her name down for a flat. I don't know what to do, I feel really sorry for her. She just puts a brave face on it though and tells me not to worry about her, but I do. She's my Mum, what else am I supposed to do?

Dear Diary,

Back on nights now. I'm pretty bored. I might watch a DVD.

Dear Diary,

When I got up today Shell was in. When I asked her why she was home, she just broke down and started crying.

The doctors have said that there's nothing more they can do for Jamie. He's gonna die, and now it's just waiting.

I asked how long he's got and apparently it could be months or even years, they just don't know.

The hospital has put Stacey and Karl in touch with a children's hospice, 'cos they can't really have him at home.

I can't believe it.

Anyway, gonna go and do, whatever, something, I don't know.

Dear Diary,

I know it's been a couple of days but it has just been shit. We went to see Jamie at the hospice.

Basically it's a place where children go to die. The sole purpose of the place is to make their last remaining days as happy as possible. They look after the parents as well, give them time to do things that they wouldn't normally get a chance to do. People say that having kids is one of the best things you can do in life.

I feel so sorry for Karl and Stacey. They are both putting a brave face on it, but when you talk to them it's like someone has ripped them apart on the inside. It's in their eyes.

We had a walk round the place and they have all these special rooms, with lights and things, for the disabled kids. I don't know how to put it into words. The job that the place does, and all the staff, it's just . . . just pure good. They take people in who have no reason to laugh or smile ever again, and they give them memories – happy memories that they can treasure forever.

Jamie was asleep when we got there, so we didn't have a chance to talk. But we saw him.

I didn't think it was him at first. He looked so different, so ill. The chemo has made him lose his hair, so he wears a cap most of the time.

That poor little boy. Why? He's never done anything to anyone. Why? It makes no sense.

I had to leave, I had to be on my own for bit, so I said I was gonna go for some fresh air. Then on the way out I passed a small chapel they have. I took a look inside and no one was there, so I went in and I did something I haven't done for a long time, I prayed.

I said, "Dear Lord, I know it's been a while, but I need your help. I know you helped me out last time but I need another favour. There's this little boy, Jamie. He has never done anything wrong; he's a good boy. And I don't want you to take him, no one does. Please Lord, spare his life. You can have mine, you must know the things I've done, please Lord, take me instead. Please don't make that little boy and his Mum and Dad suffer, they are good people and they don't deserve this. Why Lord? Why? He's just a little boy. I know I don't deserve any help from you, but I'm not asking for me this time, please Lord, make him better. Amen."

Then I went back in to see Jamie. We stayed for a bit then came home.

I think Shell wants to go back tomorrow.

Dear Diary,

It's Kev's anniversary today. I can't believe it's been two years. I miss him loads. He was my best friend and a good man. He was always there for me. It should have been me. Not him.

God, I just feel so shitty and low. I was gonna give his Mum a call but then, why would she want to hear from me? I was a soldier and it's because her son was one that he died. I just wanna curl up and sleep forever.

What's the point? Kev's dead, Jamie's dying, my family's gone and the woman I love can't stand me. Some life, this is.

Anyway, we are off to the hospice, so see you in a bit.

Dear Diary,

When we got to the hospice Jamie was awake this time. It absolutely broke my heart. He must be in so much pain. All the stuff he has to go through, every day.

He hasn't changed much; he's still into all the super heroes. I took him some of my old comics, which he really liked. Then when Shell and Karl and Stacey went for a brew, I stayed with him. We were having a laugh and I asked him what his favourite toy was and he smiled and pulled out an HM armed forces action figure, an infantryman. He said that it was his favourite 'cos this toy was a real hero, not like Superman. I nearly broke down right then and there. Then he asked me what was in all the pouches on the figure's webbing, so I went through it with him.

He told me that he always wanted to be a soldier when he grew up, "Just like you, Uncle Tommy."
So I told him that he still could.

He just said, as cool as a cucumber, "Uncle Tommy, I'm not gonna grow up, I'm gonna die soon and go to heaven."

My heart shattered into a million pieces. And then he still managed to smile, to laugh. He still managed to play and read his comics. I have seen some brave things in my time, but nothing, and I mean nothing compares to how brave that kid is.

Then they all came back in and Jamie had to go to bed. Then we came home.

I feel really ashamed. I feel like I have let everybody down. If a seven-year-old boy can face up to what's happening to him and still smile, then I can to. Sod it, so what I have nightmares, they are only bad dreams, I still get to wake up. And yeah, I miss my friends that have died, that's just natural.

Anyway, when we got in, Shell told me that Jamie hasn't got long and that Karl and Stacey want to take him to Florida, to Disneyworld, before he's too ill to travel.

The only problem is, it's gonna cost them a fortune, and because they are both off work at the minute they just can't afford it. They're thinking of getting a loan.

So I started to think and then it hit me. There's a marathon coming up in town. People do it for charity all the time.

I might not be able to cure cancer, I might not be the smartest guy on earth, but if it's one thing I can do it's bloody run. I was trained by the finest army on the planet, I could do some civvy run with a hangover and a fag in my mouth. And I swear to God, if it's the last thing I do, that little kid is going to see the mouse.

JUNE

Dear Diary,

Just got back in from training. God, I'm out of shape.
Getting better every day, though. The run's in a couple
of weeks and I've nearly got the money. I've been going
for runs round the wood near us. It's good. I've been
enjoying it, but what is it with these people who think their
professional athletes, with all the gear and stuff. Why do
they feel the need to run around in tight vests and lycra
leggings? What's wrong with a normal t-shirt and shorts?
Who do they think they are? Linford-bloody-Christie? No.
With an iPod strapped to their arm and a Hi Vis vest and
the cool trainers that some men's magazine told them to
buy? No mate, it's not a fashion show – no amount of cool
stuff will stop you breathing out of your arse and sweating
your knackers off. 'Cos that's what training is. It's there to
get you fit. Not get you a shag.

The gym is worse though. My God, I got a month's
membership; what a bunch of tossers.

I was doing some weights and there was this guy, a
big fucker, stood in front of the mirror lifting weights and
checking out his muscles.

*Oh yeah, I'm a real man, check me out, I look like a lobster,
but hey the ladies dig it.*

No mate, no. Go have a protein shake and some more
steroids. Wanker.

And why is it when you go to the gym it's like some
bloody competition? I warmed up on the running machine
and this fool came on the machine next to me and straight
away went for a sprint. I clocked him checking out what
level I was on, so I just stayed doing my own thing, nice
and gentle, with the flash next to me. He lasted about five
minutes.

The changing room is the worst bit. I know we are all blokes and it's nothing none us have never seen before but Jesus, put it away mate, stop leaning over the bench, I do not want to know what you had for breakfast, thanks.

The pensioners are the worst, they do not give a fuck, one of them stood there, one leg on the bench, letting his dongle flap about like a rusty turd, just talking to his mate cool as you like.

So anyway, that's what I've been up to. Me and Shell haven't been getting on at all, she's turned into a right moody cow. Always nagging me about the housework and shit. Er, priorities, darling. But no.

Dear Diary,

Been on days today, got some of the people in the office to sponsor me. They've been really generous: Graham gave me fifty quid, which set the standard and I'm almost there.

I went out for a fag and got a load of money. Wankers. There were a bunch of them chatting shit about something and then one of the girls came out as well, have they never seen a girl before, ogling her and checking her out, I bet she felt really uncomfortable. Animals. It pissed me right off, if you're gonna perve, then do it with some bloody tact. They made it so obvious, she's not a piece of meat, assholes, she does the same job as you, so she must have a brain. God.

But then, the top she was wearing didn't do her any good. Put 'em away, luv. I mean, if she doesn't want people to look, why wear revealing clothes?

Anyway, gotta go now. I have to put tea on.

Dear Diary,

Why are women so hard to live with?

Dear Diary,

Back on nights, thank god. Some peace and quiet for a change.

"Don't leave your shoes there. Put that away. Put the washing on. Don't leave the seat up."

Good God, woman, leave me alone, bloody wench.

I had a shave before and nearly shredded my face off. The blade was as sharp as a plastic bag. Get your own razor, stop using mine. Legs and armpit hair all over the place, I'm glad she has her bits waxed.

Anyway I'm chuffed I'm on nights. I've been doing loads of reading lately about all sorts of shit that never really interested me before.

This country is mad. The Westminster system is crazy.

I always thought that to be an MP then you had to be clever. Or at least have some knowledge of something. 'Cos at the end of the day, when you're an MP you get to make decisions that affect millions of people. So you would have thought that parliament would be full of people who knew what they were talking about.

But no. In this country, all you need to be an MP is to be over eighteen and not have a criminal record. You get that when your elected, fiddling cunts.

And that's it. Well, No wonder the country is in the shit. We have a bunch of mutants running the show.

All you have to do is pick a party, and it doesn't matter which one, 'cos to me they all the same anyway. You're best off going to the one who's won in your area, like in mine, the same party has been in since God knows when. So then you get in with the local branch.

And all you have to do is kiss their arse and go leafleting and what not, for a few years, get them to nominate you and you're in. You don't even have to be able to string a sentence together according to the rules.

And then if you do get in: this is my favourite part. If you fall out with the party you can piss off and join the other side. What?

Crossing the floor, what's that about? Apparently Churchill did it twice. But hey, that's Churchill, a double hard bastard. He could do what he wanted.

If I had voted for someone and I agreed with the stuff that the party wanted to do, I would go ape if the cheeky bastard went to the other side.

How is that right, or fair? You vote on what you believe in. Vote for a party that says it will cut tax for low earners and then your MP joins the idiots who want to raise it. Democracy, PMPL [Ed: piss my pants laughing].

Anyway gonna go have a fag outside 'cos the men in London say I have to, because as a people we can't have a room where smokers can go, because apparently people cannot read any more and a non-smoker might walk in and die.

Dear Diary,

I have just been informed that I am going out for dinner with Shell's friend and her boyfriend. And I have been told that I will be nice and I will be on my best behaviour.

And if I can't stand them, tough. I will be nice. Where's Lincoln when you need him?

Dear Diary,

Why? Why? Why, am I constantly forced to spend time with idiots? Is it so evil to want to talk about something other than the Soaps? It's not real, but tell that to the morons and they bloody cry.

So I had to sit there all night listening to the drivel that Shell and her friend Lucy were talking about. Which left me to try and talk to Josh or "Joshua" as Lucy calls him. Yes, Lucy, we have all seen fucking Friends and no, you are certainty not Rachel: she never went to weight watchers did she?

And fucking 'Joshua' is not as clean-cut as Lucy and Shell seem to think he is. The way Shell talked about him you would think that he shits gold nuggets and his sweat smells like *CK1*. But no, good old Joshua is a knob.

If you do not want to be with someone, don't be with them. I don't really like Lucy but, My God, she deserves better than him. The scumbag actually started chatting up a girl at the bar when we went to get some drinks.

And his response?

"Well you're a man of the world, Tommy. You know how it is, don't you?"

Er, no, I don't.

So he said, "Come on, all the times you were away, you never strayed?"

No, I didn't fuck tart. I love Shell and would never hurt her. If you want to shag about why have a girlfriend?

Shell thinks this prick is wonderful: "Oh, he's a director of his own firm." Yeah, OK. Turns out he works for his Dad, at the family firm.

Oh yeah, and his flash car? Daddy bought it him.

So yeah, this cunt's a real Alan Sugar.

Anyway, at some point during the evening, Lucy and Shell decided that we should go on holiday as a foursome and like an imbecile I wasn't listening, so I just agreed.

So the girls are gonna book it next week. Christ they got a bit giddy, the pair of them. I thought Edward Cullen had walked in, the way they were screaming.

They want to go to Turkey. Great. I've never been to a hot country full of Muslims before. Oh, the joy.

Dear Diary,

Absolutely buzzin'. Got the money for Jamie. Brilliant. There's enough to send the three of them to Disneyworld for ten days, plus some spending money. Now all I have to do is the marathon. Well it's only a half marathon but sod it. I can't wait to see their faces.

This feels so good. I feel like I have a purpose again. I might do some volunteering for some charities, help them out with whatever.

God, I'm in such a good mood.

Dear Diary,

The electric company are absolute wankers. Three hundred quid bill – for what? Do they think we have a runway in the garden that we have to light?

And then when you ring them to sort it out, Good God! I want to sort out my bill not kill you and your family. Jesus Christ, the way they speak to you. Oh, sorry to keep you from whatever it is you'd rather be doing, pricks. Bloody call centres. And that's after you've been on hold for twelve years.

I wouldn't mind but we told them when we moved in and gave them a metre reading. But no, obviously it's too difficult for them to do basic mathematics and work out our bill. Jesus.

So I get off the phone and of course there she is, arms

folded, face like a fart, "Why do you get so angry? There's no need for it Tommy, you're gonna have a heart attack." Good. I hope I do, then maybe I'll get to eat some decent bloody food, who the hell can't cook pasta anyway, I mean how, how can you burn pasta? Christ.

So once again I'm sleeping on the couch, because the fucking electric company failed GCSE maths. Great.

Dear Diary,

Something well weird happened to me today. It has proper freaked me out. I was doing a patrol at work and then, I was just back there. It was so real, I was back with Kev, I was holding him, telling him he was gonna be OK, begging him to stay awake.

I could smell everything, see everything, hear everything. It only lasted a few seconds but fucking hell, I went to the toilet and I nearly threw up. I was white as a fucking sheet.

Fucking flashbacks now? Why have I never had them before? I thought it was supposed to get better over time not worse.

I don't know what to do, I can't tell anybody, there'll put me away in the looney bin.

I'm afraid. What if it happens again?

Dear Diary,

It's been a couple of days, but after my little trip down memory lane at work I just haven't wanted to write.

Anyway, it hasn't happened again and hopefully it won't.

Well, let me catch you up. We are off to Turkey next month, yippee! A week with the light of my life and her chums.

So now I have to get all new clothes. Wonderful, another trip to the shopping centre. Least Frodo and Sam only had to go to Mordor once.

Anyway, gonna go download some music so I can drown out the world.

Dear Diary,

Karl and Stacey were over the moon. Jamie's face was just excellent. Even Shell said she was proud of me. We had a bit when we got home. I had forgotten what it was like.

Anyway, I'm buzzin' my tits off. They are all gonna come and see me do the run, they even want to bring Jamie if he's well enough. Can't wait. I might even do it dressed up.

Dear Diary,

At work, I'm bored. God, it goes slow sometimes on nights. I've just finished reading a book by a guy called Joseph Conrad. Jesus, he was a happy-go-lucky fella. Graham put me on to it; he said that this book is what *Apocalypse Now* was based on. What? How has Vietnam got anything to do with the Congo? God, it was depressing. No one in that book was smelling anything in the morning let alone bloody napalm. Good film that though. *Charlie don't surf.* Excellent.

Anyway gonna go for a mooch round, see if I can spot any natives being naughty outside.

Dear Diary,

Jamie's dead.

When I got in from work Shell was on the couch; she looked like a panda. I asked her what was wrong and she just said, "Jamie died in the early hours of this morning," and that was it.

We didn't speak for ages. I don't think either of us knew what to say. Shell has known Stacey for years: they went to school together. I didn't know what to say or do.

When someone died over there, we just got on with it. We still had a job to do. But now? I've just been in a trance all day.

That little boy. Dead. Seven years old.

All he wanted to do was read comics and play with his toys. Was that too much to ask? Why? A child. A fucking child.

He's never gonna grow up. He's not gonna go to High School. He will not get a chance at life. Now he's never gonna fall in love, or get drunk, or any of it.

And now two good people have to bury their only son.

They have to put him in a box and put him in the ground.

They have never broken the law, they both work hard and pay their taxes. Why?

That poor, brave little boy. All the pain he had to go through and so quickly. You hear about people lasting years that have cancer.

Jamie didn't even have enough time to go and see Mickey Mouse. He would have liked that, it would have made him happy, for a little bit at least. It would have given them a last chance at being a family, together, smiling, happy, just one last time.

And now they are never gonna see their son ever again. There never gonna kiss him goodnight or read him a story. They won't get to cuddle him when he's frightened or tell him off when he's naughty.

Now they're not gonna get the chance to see him get married or have kids of his own. Why? Seven years old.

I hope one day, somebody, somewhere, finds a cure for this, this evil.

The hardest thing I have ever done is watch a parent bury their child. Heart-breaking doesn't even begin to cover it and this time it's a little boy. He won't even have a full-size coffin.

I think I'm gonna have a drink now. See you soon.

Dear Diary,

I know I haven't wrote for ages. I didn't want to. I couldn't get the words. It's his funeral tomorrow.

Me and Shell went to the hospice to see him.

Whenever a child dies there, they have a special room where they put them until the funeral. Like at a funeral director's when you go and see the body and it is in a coffin.

But this room is like a kid's bedroom. They're not in a coffin, they put them in a bed. So it's like they are asleep. So we went in and the first thing that hits you is the cold. It's very dark, but we sat next to his bed and he looked so peaceful. So sweet. Just asleep. Forever.

They had put all his favourite toys in there, so he wouldn't be on his own. He was cuddling a Mickey Mouse teddy bear, 'cos he had it since he was a baby.

And on the bedside table was the infantryman, standing watch over him.

Shell held his little hand. She sobbed her heart out. She was there on the day he was born.

I couldn't even bring myself to touch him. I tried but he was so cold, I couldn't do it.

Anyway gonna go now, got a day tomorrow.

Dear Diary,

What a day. It was horrible. When we were getting ready this morning, I kept listening to *The Show Must Go On* by Queen, on my iPod. Quite fitting really, given the circumstances. I love that song. I listened to it after Kev died and Johno and the Sarge.

When I left the army I thought I would never have to listen to it again.

Anyway, Karl and Stacey didn't want anyone to wear black, at all. They wanted it to be a celebration of his short life.

He had a little baby blue coffin. Karl carried it in all by himself. There wasn't a dry eye in the place.

I can't describe the respect and affection I felt for them. They were so brave. But then at the end when they played *You've Got A Friend In Me* from *Toy Story* and the curtains closed, Stacey tried to go and get her son. "That's my baby, my boy," she screamed.

Karl pulled her away and just hugged her.

I don't remember much after that. It was a funeral. So we said our goodbyes to Karl and Stacey then headed home.

We had tea and watched some telly. I can't stop thinking about them. What are they doing tonight? Are they watching telly, I mean, what do you do?

Anyway Shell went to bed early. So I went to go and see Kev. I needed a friend. I needed someone to tell me everything was gonna be OK.

When I got there the place was deserted as usual, apart from a couple of tramps sleeping on the benches.

And I just talked to him for a bit, I said, "Hi mate. Sorry I've not been for a bit. I always think of you though. I miss you. I know, I'm goin' soft – what do you expect, I'm a civvy now, with a suit and everything. I came because I need a favour. There's a little boy, Jamie. I want you to look after him for me. He's only seven and he's gonna need someone to look out for him up there. I know you will, mate, and I promise I will go down to your grave and give you a pint. And, so you know, from where I'm standing I can see the flag, it's still flying mate, we did our job. Anyway gonna go now."

As I was walking away from the cenotaph, all that went through my head was that song and Freddie's words.

I'll face it with a grin, I'm never givin' in.
The show must go on.

JULY

Dear Diary,

Well it's nearly time. The things booked and there's no escape. We fly in a couple of days. Tonight is my last night at work for a bit.

We asked Karl and Stacey if they wanted to come, but it's just too soon. Can't blame them, really. I'm fine and I don't want to go.

I've not had any nightmares or any more flashbacks for a bit. I still have trouble sleeping. I'm just tired all the time; it's like having permanent jet lag.

Anyway, gonna go finish my book. I'm reading a book of my Dad's, called *Flashman*; it's about a Victorian soldier. Oh My God, it's well funny, I haven't laughed like that for a long time. Good old Flashy, what a rake. I think I'm gonna buy a couple more for the holiday: I'd rather be at Balaclava with Flashman than in Turkey with these people.

Anyway, gonna go have a fag.

Dear Diary,

We fly tomorrow. Lucy and 'Joshua' are staying at ours, we've got a taxi booked for the morning, at silly o'clock. They are all really giddy. You'd think none of them had flown before.

Anyway, gonna go and try and get some sleep.

Dear Diary,

Well, we're here. What a joke. Next time I fly I'm goin' private. It's ridiculous. Are they taking the piss? Seriously, have they all got together and said, "I know, let's take something that people look forward to for ages, that they wait for all year and then lets mess them about and make them suffer. Ha, ha."

So the taxi got there no problem. We were nice and early and me in my blissful ignorance thought that the airport would be quiet. But no. Bugger me, the entire human race was flying today, good God the queues for the check-in were out the door.

So we dutifully lined up with all the other sheep and were herded towards the desk.

There was a family in front of us, My God, sort your kids out. Jesus. Extras from *Jeremy Kyle*, these. Speak some form of English you ignorant idiot.

And then after a week we got to the desk and the absolutely lovely woman who checked us in. More make-up than boots, this one.

Then, *then* you get the questions: "Have you packed yourself, sir?"

No, my friend Osama did it for me.

"Has anybody tampered with your luggage?"

Oh yeah, the taxi driver put something in, some vial of liquid.

"Has anybody given you anything to carry?"

Yeah, my mate Carlos gave me a big bag of white powder. Dicks.

Why would anybody not say 'no' to those questions? I'm all for tight security but there's no need to be stupid about it. Common sense? Nothing common about it, it's rarer than rocking horse shit.

Anyway so we finally get rid of our bags and go through security. Well it's not really security it's a mugging. Thieving bastards.

So, after another week of queuing up we get to check-point Charlie. I'm surprised the idiots who searched us didn't goose-step up and down the place. Fascist bastards.

So we put our hand baggage through the machine. Those three got through fine. Then it's me. I got through fine: the machine didn't go off, but I still got wanded and had to take my shoes off. Do I look like a terrorist, mate? These morons wouldn't know a terrorist if one ran behind them and shouted Allah [Ed: illegible word] Akbar.

And then they searched my bag.
"Do you know that you can't take this through sir?"
What, some aftershave? What am I gonna do with that: "This is a hi-jacking nobody move or I'll make you smell nice." Piss off.

So the bastards stole, fucking stole my sixty quid aftershave and it wasn't just me, there was loads and I mean loads of products and toiletries and all other kinds of shit in a big bin behind the desk.

What . . . the . . . hell. How is that legal? How is that right? I asked when I could get it back and they said never, it's been confiscated. What, am I at school? CONFISCATED! It's my personal property dickhead and I want it back when I get home, but you don't apparently 'cos it's the law.

Did we lose the war? Is my history wrong? Five years and God knows how many lives to stop the Nazis, to make sure we had our freedoms and now we get this?

It's a racket, that's what it is. All these mutants are making a killing with this stuff; well, the fat paedo-looking one who stole my aftershave is gonna smell nice for his cats tonight, anyway.

Shell said it was my own fault, I should have read the security signs. And what I was wearing didn't help. What? A pair of shorts and an England shirt. She said, "You look like a hooligan." Do I 'eck, I look like I'm goin' on holiday.

Then the penny dropped. What do you walk through after you have been through the Reich? Oh yeah, Duty Free. Terrorism, safety, security my arse. They take all your shit so you buy more from them, and they are allowed to do this under the guise of protection? Well, Rule Britannia.

So they went for some food. I went for a fag and froze

my tits off. When they called our flight everyone was under the impression that if they got to the front of the queue the plane would somehow take off sooner. No. It's not going anywhere until everyone is on board, knobheads.

Anyway gonna go and go sleep, 'cos I've got a busy day at the beach tomorrow. Can't wait.

Dear Diary,

Just got back from the beach. Shell's in the shower. What a day. The hotel is nice enough, it's got its own pool and what not and the bar's nice. Three hours in a bus though with a load of Sweaty Betties who had been up all day. Nice.

Anyway, we went down for breakfast this morning and who should be there, only the same family who pissed me off at the airport, Mr and Mrs Mutant and their five kids, well actually I think one of the spawn might be a grandkid, 'cos their daughters all look like they believe in no sex before marriage.

So we had breakfast, continental and some other shit. The hotel is packed with Brits – would some corn flakes or a full English be out of the question? Who has ham for breakfast and cheese anyway? No wonder we had the largest empire and ruled the waves, we didn't eat like morons.

So then, after breakfast we got ready and went down to the beach. Now according to Shell and Lucy the hotel is only a few minutes away from the beach. That is true. If you take a taxi.

So we set off walking with the bags and everything and twenty minutes later we finally got to the beach.

Then we had to find a spot, not just any spot, oh no: the girls wanted something special. It was like an episode of *Location, Location, Location*.

So while the girls were sunbathing, me and Josh went for a swim. Well, we just bobbed along like a couple of turds, but hey.

You know I was starting to warm to him a little bit, after all, who else was I gonna talk to?

Then out of nowhere he just said, "Look at that filthy bastard."

So I said, "Who?"

"Him over there! Who the fuck does he think he is?"

So I just asked him who he was talking about.

"That filthy nigger over there."

I swear to God I nearly drowned; I swallowed a load of water and was coughing my guts up. bloody salt.

So then he carries on with himself, "It's disgusting one of them with a white girl, it shouldn't be allowed."

Turns out good old Joshua is only a card-carrying member of the BN fucking P.

I hated him when he was just a cunt. But then he started telling me about his 'views' and his 'political activities'. Ignorant fucking prick.

I may not have a degree in biology but I know that the colour of someone's skin is determined by how much melanin you have in your body, and that's it.

It's like saying that I hate someone because they have blonde hair, or green eyes. How does that make anyone better or worse? It's just biology.

The truth is there are knobheads of every colour, every age, men, women, gay, straight. It's personality that counts not something so superficial as skin colour.

But this idiot was having none of it, said I was brainwashed by society.

So anyway I just said, "Look mate, you can think whatever you want, but don't spout your shit off round me, OK?"

So we agreed to disagree and left it at that.

Well, I did have a sneaky piss when I was swimming next to him, ha.

Dear Diary,

I might swap Shell for a camel and a Ted Baker top. She thinks that knob is so wonderful.

"Oh, he treats Lucy so nice and he's very polite, so well mannered."

What?

"Don't they make a lovely couple, he'd walk over hot coals for her."

Yeah, to get to somebody else, the scumbag.

Fucking hell, can nobody see he's a wanker. Why do women fall for it?

Oh yeah, 'cos he's good looking and has money and his vocabulary includes please and thank you. Feminism, my arse.

Anyway, we are all going out tonight so I have to get ready and wear something nice, not shorts though because it's far too cold here for that.

Dear Diary,

Had a really nice time tonight, until the drinking started. We went for a meal at this place we found today, traditional Turkish food. I ordered this thing, god knows what it was, but when they brought it out it was on fire and it was massive.

We all got really pissed, then went to a club. That sleaze couldn't keep his eyes of anything that moved though, Jesus Christ mate, your bird is over there. Lucy might be a bit overweight and a knob but no one deserves to be treated like that, she might be a moose but she can do better than him.

Anyway, then to top it all we nearly got into a fight. With a load of gay lads. How mad is that? All because that knob was born in the wrong bloody century.

I don't know what he said to them but they went
ballistic, God it was funny, I've never seen gay guys kick off
before.
"Come on then, dickhead, I'll knock you out." Only they
said it as camp as a row of tents. I was quite happy to let
this little adventure play itself out, but then one of them
grabbed a bottle, so I just pulled Joshua out of there.

So of course those two are all over him when we got
outside, "Are you OK, God you're so brave, standing up to
four of them on your own."

WHAT! Standing up to who? He did nowt, the prick.
He was shitting himself. And the best bit: "Where were you,
Tommy? Why didn't you help him?"

I've changed my mind; I'll give the Turks a Ted Baker
top, and my bloody iPod.

Dear Diary,

We are gonna spend the day by the pool. Why? Well
it's fun sitting in the sun all day to try and get a tan. And,
irony of ironies, who wants to turn their skin a darker
colour, the most? Only the fucking Führer. With his carrot
oil and Ray-Bans. That made me smile, he wants to be
careful, they might kick him out if he tans too much.

So while the three amigos are cooking I'm gonna sit
at the bar and read *Flashman*. Least when he's a cad and a
rake it's funny.

Dear Diary,

I'm now officially celibate. Because the woman I love decided it would be a good idea to fall asleep by the pool, in 98 degree heat. So now I have to go out and find an industrial supply of aloe bloody vera.

Jesus she looks like someone's picked her out of a tank.

Dear Diary,

We went out again tonight. Not far though 'cos "Sebastian the crab" couldn't walk that far. I went down to the bar to wait for the girls 'cos Lucy said idiot boy was already down there.

So I walked towards the bar and who should be chatting up a Russian bird? He was even feeling her ass, so I just walked past and shoved him in the pool.

"Oh, terribly sorry, old chum, didn't see you there."

He told Shell and Lucy that he slipped in. Ha.

Then we went out and had some food. We came back early and just went to bed.

Dear Diary,

I couldn't sleep, so I got up and read for a bit. *Flashman* makes me piss. I've learned more about history from reading them books than I ever did at school. It's absolutely mad, we ran the whole world, we were bastards, but hey, we were better at it than the yanks.

Anyway I finished the book and just sat there,

watching the sun rise. You don't appreciate how beautiful some things can be, until it might be your last one, I watched every sunset and sunrise whenever I could out there. 'Cos any time it could have been my last.

Anyway, gonna go have a shower.

Dear Diary,

The lunatics I'm with have only gone and made friends with Mr and Mrs Mutant.

I was late going down for breakfast and when I walked into the restaurant, oh My God, they were all sat together. All dead friendly.

Jesus Christ, I wanted to puke. None of them work; they are all on benefits and are they ashamed? Are they balls. They were telling Shell and Lucy how much they got and how to do it. I have to admit even Josh looked disgusted; so much for the Aryan race, hey, mate.

But oh, of course neither of them can work; she's got dodgy hips and knees and needs them replacing – no wonder, you look like Jabba the Hutt, lose some weight and your knees might not give out under the strain. He's got a bad back, funny that, it didn't bother him when he was on the jet skis yesterday, did it?

Oh, but of course they are both on Facebook, she's on it all day apparently. So why can't you work in an office then, knobhead? But oh no, they're entitled to it, aren't they.

That's what pisses me of the most, they think for some reason that they are entitled to it. They're so fucking special that they don't have to work. Her Majesty's government and by proxy everybody who pays tax will look after them and put food on their table and pay for their holidays and big screen TVs and X-boxes for their useless kids.

And their kids. The eldest, only seventeen, has two kids to two different Dads, I saw her eyeing up Josh and the prick did the same. I won't tell him that the CSA are worse than Dracula, blood-sucking bastards. Go on mate do it, fifteen minutes with a trout and then eighteen years and two thirds of everything you earn, a third for the sprog and then a third for her, so she can sit on her ass and pay for her bad fake nails and eye lashes, hair extensions and fake tan. It happened to loads of guys I know, all for a bit of crap pussy.

No princess, you might have had a nice body once, but after two kids no one wants to see your stretch marks, put yourself away. Jesus.

How the hell can these people afford to come on holiday?

They should take their fucking passports off them, what do they need one for? If you're out of work then you should be looking for job. But no, they're not well enough to work.

So, how about the guys who come back with no legs or arms or worse and then climb mountains and run marathons? They still work and pay their way.

But these things: fucking worthless scum.

The sad fact is they are too stupid and ignorant to comprehend what they are.

Anyway, after breakfast we all went for a boat trip, all we did was sail around the coast and stop every now and again so people could swim. All day.

I'm gonna go and get smashed.

Dear Diary,

Last day today, thank god I've been hung over for most of the day so I just slept under a brolly on the beach, while they were doing, whatever.

Anyway it's not been that bad, it's another stamp on my passport.

Gonna go pack.

Dear Diary,

Just got back home. We didn't arrive until late. I'm really tired and can't be arsed doing anything.

The airport when we got back was a nightmare. One hour and twenty minutes from getting off the plane to getting to the baggage collection point.

Four flights landed at the same time and how many desks were open at passport control? THREE! Oh, they apologised for the delay, apparently they weren't expecting so many flights. REALLY! All last minute were they? Didn't know they were coming did they? No, well, we knew weeks ago the date and time we were flying. How rude, Thomas Cook forgot to tell the airport. Idiots.

Shell has been in a right mood all the way back. What for, I don't know. I haven't done anything to upset her, although these days all I have to is breathe and it pisses her off.

When we got back in I tried to be nice to her, but she was having none of it.

She just said, "Not now Tommy, I'm not in the mood, but tomorrow we need to talk."

That's never good, is it?

AUGUST

Dear Diary,

I've been given my orders. Sort myself out or it's over. Cheeky bitch. Who the fuck does she think she is?

Sort myself out! What for? There's nothing wrong with me, it's her, the moose. I wish God had given us a mute button for them, bloody split arses.

She said I was a complete dick when we went away, and Lucy and Josh don't like me. Well boo fucking hoo, pass some tissues while I have a cry. She said Lucy thinks I'm really ignorant 'cos I didn't talk to her much and I made everyone feel uncomfortable when I was about. WHAT! And then Josh apparently said that he doesn't know what Shell is doing with me, 'cos she can do better.

That just priceless. What a knob. I've killed better men than that prick and he's got the balls to judge me? The worse thing is Shell listens to these cunts. What do they know? Wankers. Telling Shell to finish with me.

Anyway, so we are gonna try and sort it out, how I don't know, 'cos I have no idea what she wants from me.

Dear Diary,

Back at work now, straight on to nights. Just finished a patrol. I spoke to my Dad before; his wedding is in a couple of weeks. I think I will be his Best Man – I hope I don't have to give a speech.

Anyway, I was at the shops before to get some bits and this poor woman had a pram and a load of bags. She couldn't get the things down the steps and dropped all her shopping. So I gave her lift with the pram and her bags, and she said, "Oh, thanks, not many like you about, is there?" I wondered what she meant and then I realised that there were loads of people just stood about doing bugger all. Not being funny but how can you not stop and help someone? What is wrong with people, it was well weird, when I first went over she looked dead sacred, like a rabbit in headlights, but then she was fine.

So anyway, gonna go, I bought the next *Flashman* today.

Dear Diary,

Went and saw my Mum today. God she's a mess. She's not looking after herself and the house is a shit hole. I tidied up for her and cleaned the place up.
 She said, "You don't have to do this, Tommy, it'll be all right," so I just said, "Mum, you can't live like this, and how are you gonna sell the house in this state?"

So then she went mad at me, "I'm bloody depressed, Tommy, I don't know what to do, we were married twenty-five years and he just fucks off with another woman."

"Here," she said, "Look, *look* – this is how depressed I am," and she threw a noose she had made at me.

A bloody noose! She wanted to hang herself. I had no idea she was that bad. Bloody hell.

So I went over and gave her a hug. I said, "Don't worry Mum, it'll be all right, I promise. It just takes time, that's all. You never know you might even get a toy boy."

She laughed at that.

So I hid the noose in my bedroom. I'm dead worried about her, she's drinking way too much. That's all I need, another looney to deal with. Women! Head cases, all of them.

Dear Diary,

Fucking England, useless bastards. Can't even win a friendly against a bunch of cave dwellers. Wankers.

How hard is it? Get paid more money than God to kick a piece of leather round a field two or three times a week and then every once in while you get asked to play for your country and these mongs just stand there like fucking idiots.

"Da doh, da fuutboll want wong waayy."

I wouldn't mind but everyone I know would wear an England shirt for free. Christ, a lot would pay to do it and these morons just laugh at us.

Christ we'll win another fucking world war before we get the World Cup back. Wankers.

People work their bollocks off to pay a ridiculous amount of money to see them play every week and then the one time the whole country is united in one common cause, the dickheads let us all down. I've had skid marks with more fucking brain cells. Cunts.

The beautiful game, my fucking arse.

Dear Diary,

Had another flashback today, this one was a firefight. It's so horrible. I think I'm going mad. I don't want this any more. I haven't told anyone. Not my Mum or Dad or Shell. What do I say? I can't say anything.

It's my own fault anyway, I volunteered. Hey, you reap what you sow, don't you?

Fuck it.

Dear Diary,

At my Dad's tonight; he gets married again tomorrow. I can't sleep, just got loads of stuff floating round my head.

I keep thinking of Jamie. All the stuff he will never do. And my Mum and Dad, it just feels so weird. I feel so alone. My Dad's moved on, my Mum's found the bottle. What do I do?

Fuck it, you come in to this world alone and you go out of it alone; the rest is just filler.

I don't want to lose Shell, she's my world. I just don't know what she wants any more. I don't hit her, I don't treat her bad, I hardly go out, I don't chase other girls and I don't piss my money up the wall. What does she want from me?

Yeah. I get pissed off and angry, it's not that bad, is it? I'm not mad at her, half the time I'm not even speaking to her, I just shout at no one, just vent.

Normal people don't do that, do they though, she says. Well, I'm not normal, am I? I'm a freak who's lost his marbles: nightmares and flashbacks. I thought I was stronger than that. I thought I was a good soldier. Obviously not.

I'm not even a soldier any more, am I, just a nobody, just a weirdo.

I should have died over there. Then at least I would be remembered, my life would have meant something, people would have said nice things about me. Now no one even likes me. They don't say it but I feel it: the elephant in the room.

Anyway, got a busy day tomorrow.

Dear Diary,

Bloody hell, what a day. It's been brilliant. Jesus Christ. This morning we got up and had breakfast, then we went to the Registry Office. Shell and Ian met us there and everyone else started turning up, I met Lisa's Mum and Dad: ancient they were.

Anyway, we had the ceremony, standard shit. Then went back to the room they had hired at a hotel.

I was starting to get really nervous now 'cos of my speech. So I had a couple of JDs straight and smoked like a trooper.

The meal was lovely, minted lamb. So then it was time for my speech.

Bloody hell, I thought I was gonna spew, I was so nervous. I well thought I was going to freeze and bottle it.

Anyway, everybody loved it; my Dad cried, the big gay bear.

"Did you write that yourself, Tommy?" everyone asked.

"Yeah it took me ages, I wanted to get it just right."

God bless the internet. My God. I Googled 'Best Man' speeches and managed to cobble it together.

It was a good day; me and Shell were getting on mint. We had a really good time.

Then later on after the meal, my Dad and Lisa went to get changed; yeah of course they did, in the honeymoon suite, for forty-five minutes.

Anyway the DJ had pissed off for a bit to God knows where and left his stuff.

It was quite cool, he had a projector screen on stage that was showing a slide show of the photographer's pictures. It was sweet – at the bottom he had put messages from people, congratulations and shit.

He left the music on; he had it on a laptop, soppy stuff and old stuff my Dad and Lisa like.

So I was at the bar talking to some idiot, then the music went off and all I heard was a quiet, nervous laughing spread round the room.

I wondered what was going on, so I turned round and there on the big screen on the stage at the front of the room was a big cock being sucked by some woman.

The DJ only had porn on his laptop. It must have been on his media player after the playlist or something. Bloody hell, it was hilarious.

There was kids in the room, all the Mums covered their eyes, I thought Lisa's Mum was gonna have a heart attack.

Then the scene changed, a big black guy doing some girl up the arse.

So me and Ian went to try and turn it off: the funniest thing was the messages were still rolling across the screen. So you had "Congratulations Mr and Mrs Atkins, don't they make a lovely couple?" And then behind it a girl having her brains banged out by a guy. Fuck me, I haven't laughed that hard for a long time.

And then we only went and put the fucking volume on, didn't we, so now you got the soundtrack as well. The place exploded, so we ended up pulling the plug.

When the DJ came back he was mortified. He apologised to my Dad and Lisa. It was on there for when he did stag dos and things. Yeah. Sure it was, mate.

Anyway no one was too offended and saw the funny side. My sides were hurting.

Yeah it was a really good day.

Me and a Shell even had a bit when we got home.

Dear Diary,

It's gone one in the morning. I'm a waste of life. For the first time ever I raised my hand at Shell.

We were watching telly before, *Biggest Loser UK*. Absolute drivel. So I said that to lose weight you had to burn off more than you eat, it's just basic maths.

So then Shell, champion of the obese, hit the roof. "It's not their fault," she says, "some people are just naturally big."

"Naturally fucking greedy," I said.

So then it started. World War Three. We just shouted at each other for ages.

She assassinated my whole character, then I told her why she was wrong.

Then she said it, didn't she? "You're nothing but a fucking coward Tommy Atkins." And then she went for me, started hitting me and hurling abuse.

All I heard was 'coward'.

I got so angry, a different kind of angry. I pushed her off me with such force that she flew against the wall, the next thing I knew I had her by the throat with my fist raised.

Then I saw the fear in her eyes.

"Go on, do it," she said.

I let her go. Then I grabbed the car keys and left. I had to get out of there.

To where, I didn't know. I just drove. I got on the motorway and just put my foot down.

I turned the stereo right up; I listened to that *Journey* song, *Separate Ways*, and just cried my eyes out. I couldn't see for the tears.

There was no one on the road, so I sped up. Then a thought entered my head. I thought about driving off the road and ending it right there.

For a split second I did.

Then the next song came on. '*You've Got a Friend in Me*'. I made the CD ages ago. I forgot it was on there. Then I

110

slowed down and I pulled off at the next junction. I parked up and just sobbed. Just sat there and cried for what felt like hours.

When I got home I thought Shell would be in bed: she was up. She had the phone in her hand, "It's OK, he's back." She had phoned my Dad 'cos she was worried.

She told me she loved me, but I had changed. I wasn't the man she fell in love with. We hugged and made up. I apologised for everything. She said it was OK. She said it must be hard for me and that I needed to get help.

She said she'd been on a website for a thing called *Combat Stress*, a charity that helps ex-forces personnel with mental problems. I said I would give them a call.

She smiled and said, "Good, I want the man I fell in love with back."

I didn't have the heart to tell her that he was dead. That he died on some corner of a foreign field.

That he was never going to come back.

SEPTEMBER

Dear Diary,

Love *Flashman*. He's so funny. Just finished another one. I'm at work, gonna put *Doctor Who* on. Not sure about Matt Smith yet. Anyway gonna go for a fag and make a brew.

Dear Diary,

Had a horrible nightmare today. They were getting less frequent. I can't be having them again. The flashbacks are getting worse too. I had one the other day. I was just sat watching telly and it happened.

I was gonna ring that *Combat Stress*. But I bottled it. What the fuck do I say: "I'm having nightmares, help me?" They'd probably laugh.

Anyway, Shell's gone out with some friends from work. I bet that fucking Nick is there, all over her, the cunt.

I bet they're fucking laughing and flirting. "Oh Nick, you're so funny." Fucking knobs.

I bet she's with him right now. The fucking bitch.

Dear Diary,

I asked Shell who she went out with and she just said, "Oh, just me and the girls from work."
I know when someone is lying to me, so I called her on it.
"What, so you think I cheated on you with Nick?" she said.
"Well, did you?"
She flatly denied it, but I'm not sure. She says I'm fucking paranoid. But that's what you'd say, isn't it, if you were cheating on someone?

So anyway she stormed off. Knob.

Dear Diary,

In quite a good mood today. I've just downloaded the *Doctor Who* soundtracks, they're really good. Love the eleventh Doctor's theme.

Anyway, not been up to much. Work's shit, it's just the same every day, nothing ever changes, nothing ever happens. It's just boring all the time.

Dear Diary,

Me and Shell have split up. I don't know what to do. I feel like someone's punched a hole straight through me.

We were fine. Just having tea. Then we had a blazing row. Over I don't know what.

And then she just came out with it.

"It's over, Tommy. I can't do this any more. You've changed. I thought it would get better, I thought I could handle it, but I can't."

So I just said, "Fine. It's fucking over then, you know where the fucking door is."

So then, of course, she started to cry.

"That's it? Just like that? Do you even care?" she said.

"Fuck off and leave me alone if that's what you want. Go back to your parents, they'll fucking love it. Now maybe you can get with a real man, like fucking Nick," I said. Then she left. I don't know where she went.

I just went upstairs and lay on the bed for a bit.

Dear Diary,

Shell's Dad has just left with all her things. Fuck them and fuck her. She's probably with Nick, crying on his shoulder, the slag.

I'm glad, fucking glad it's over. A bit of freedom. No more nagging or rows, an easy fucking life.

Now I'm gonna go have a shower and get ready. Me and Ian are going out on the piss.

Dear Diary,

I'm back now; I'm a bit drunk. The house feels so empty. I'm gonna sleep on the couch, the bed still smells like her.

Dear Diary,

In work. Bored. Just done a patrol. I want to hate her. But I don't. I miss her. I love her. What have I done? Why didn't I fight for her? Why didn't I make her understand how I was feeling?

God, I feel like, just, low and sad. I can't stop crying. I'm so fucking soft. Jesus.

Dear Diary,

I'm moving out of the house, I've spoken to the estate agent and they said it's OK. I just can't stay there any more. Everywhere I look, it reminds me of her.

So I'm gonna move back in with my Mum. She's found a hobby; she plays darts for the local pub, so goes there every night. Good. I can't be doing with her and her shit right now.

Dear Diary,

It's silly 'o clock again. I can't sleep. I can't stop think about Shell. Where is she, what's she doing. Who's she with?

Is she in bed with someone else? Are they having sex? Is she doing the stuff she used to do with me.

I'm just so sad and low.

I love her so much. I just want to hold her again. To see her smile at me. Smell her hair and perfume.

I want to tell her to hurry up when she's getting ready to go out. I want her to shout at me for not doing the pots. I just want her back.

Why can't I be the man she fell in love with? So confident, so strong.

Well he's gone forever.

Fuck it. Fuck her, fuck her family. Fuck her friends and fuck the world.

Dear Diary,

I moved back in with Mum today. She was dead nice, made me some tea and then went out to the pub.

It's a good job I moved back in 'cos she's missed a few months' mortgage payments, drank it away probably.

Anyway it feels weird, it doesn't feel like home. My Dad's not here, the place is a mess. It just feels weird. Not real. I'm back right where I started.

OCTOBER

Dear Diary,

What the fuck is it with these banks? Cheeky bastards. Twenty-five quid just to send out a letter. Are they for real? My Direct Debit bounced 'cos, I was two quid short, so what do they do? Charge me thirty-five quid for bouncing the Direct Debit and then charge me another twenty-five quid for going over my overdraft and then charge me again for sending me a letter to tell me this.

And this is fucking legal. How the do they get away with this? Oh yeah, 'cos they all have friends in high places; the old school tie network is it? What do all these bastards down in London do? Have lunch and decide to screw over the working people, bankers and MPs they make me want to vomit.

"Oh yeah, we are all right, we earn loads of money. Let's get the people who we rely on to exist. 'Cos of course without the voters and our customers we would still be where we are." Knobheads. Selfish, greedy fucking bastards.

If it was up to me I would stab every one of those greedy bankers and fat cats once for every pound and once for every job they have cost this country, then I would drag their bodies through the streets for people to spit on. Knobs.

Then I would hang all the scumbag politicians who lined their own pockets at the taxpayers' expense and just stood by while the country was being destroyed. I would hang them all for fucking treason. Lying, low life, degenerate germs.

Where do they get the balls?

Dear Diary,

Had another nightmare, usual shit, death and violence.
Had enough.

Dear Diary,

Why are some people not worthy of the air they
breathe?
I went for a fag outside at work and then this mutant
in a car decides to share with the world his taste in music.
Yes mate, you have a stereo in your car. Well done. Is
there really any need for you to drive round in a nightclub?
No. You're a knob. Do the world a favour and go jump
under a bus. Useless fucking wanker. I could have quite
gladly put a bullet through that cunt's eyes. The prick.

Dear Diary,

Yet another fucking flashback today. Wonderful.

Dear Diary,

God, my Mum is such a knob. Go have another drink.

Dear Diary,

Saw Shell on my dinner today. She was with Nick, laughing and smiling, him and her and their chums.

It broke my heart. I wanted to go in and tell her I still loved her and wanted her back.

But fuck it, what does she want with me?

Gonna watch *Doctor Who*.

Dear Diary,

Why can't people fucking drive. Do they not have to take a fucking test? Fucking knobs. Go have a fucking crash and burn to death in agony, useless fucking cunts.

It's Give Way to the fucking right at a roundabout in this country, you fucking idiot.

And then these fucking people who should be on oxygen, what the fuck are they doing on the road, dangerous fucking idiots? You're too fucking old, do people a favour and just fucking die before you kill someone's fucking kids or take their Dad or Mum away 'cos you can't fucking see the road. Jesus Christ.

Why why, why, why, do we have to put with these cunts.

Bollocks.

Dear Diary,

Lost my job today. It was my fault. I just got really mad and lost my temper, and Graham had to sack me. Thank God, he didn't want to press charges. The poor bastard.

I was outside having a fag. I was on my own, then a few of them came out. They all started staring at me. So I said to one of them, "What the fuck are you looking at? Do you want a fucking picture?"

Then one of them said it: "Chill out, you fucking psycho."

So I went for him. I punched him in the face, then I did it again and again and again.

I don't know what happened. I just got so angry. I wasn't even angry at him. He was just there. I just wanted to destroy something.

Graham managed to persuade the guy not to press charges. Thank god one of the girls screamed, that's what snapped me out of it.

I wanted to kill the poor bastard. Why?

But Graham said he had to let me go. He said I needed help.

What does he know? Need help? An ex-copper telling me about my mind. Piss off.

Anyway, gonna go get pissed.

Fuck the world.

NOVEMBER

Dear Diary,

Sorry I haven't wrote in weeks. Just not wanted to. There's been nothing to write about.

I didn't think telling you about all the films I've watched or the music I've listened to, was that good.

Anyway, let me catch you up. I never see my Mum, she's always out at either darts or with her new fella. I don't even know his name.

Anyway, not spoken to my Dad 'cos he's a wanker. Too busy with his new wife.

The prick calls me all the time and leaves me messages. Fuck him.

And Shell is now going out with Nick. I heard off Ian. He said he saw them in town.

Not even Ian wants to know me now: he's got a new boyfriend.

So it's just me. Always. I would say I was alone but I'm not. I've my nightmares and flashbacks to keep me company. They're always good fun.

No girlfriend, no job, no friends and no family. What a life.

And this is my reward for serving my country. For killing for this country. For watching my best friend die in my arms. For seeing men blown to bits at the side of a road, little tiny pieces of brain and bone spread across my face. For what?

For nothing that's what. No one cares, too busy making money, too busy screwing each other over, selfish bastards.

How wrong was I? There was a time I was so proud to be in the army, to be a soldier. There was a time when I thought to myself: it's OK, put your kids to bed, read them a story and kiss them goodnight. Go and watch some rubbish on TV with the person you love, because nothing is going to hurt you tonight, not while we are here. As long as we are here no one will come into your home and hurt you. No one will ever take this country away from you. The flag will always fly and you will always have freedom.

What a fucking joke. How naive and innocent I was. But then I was barely shaving, was I? I learned to shoot a gun before I could even drive or vote or have a drink.

A child. That's all I was when I joined the army, a child.

But I had to grow up pretty fucking quick.

Because a bullet doesn't care how old you are. An IED doesn't care about your Mum and Dad, wife and kids. They will kill you anyway.

And then what do you get, a coffin with a tablecloth on it? A hero's welcome at Wootton Bassett? Why would you care? You're dead. You will never do anything again. Ever.

What's the fucking point?

Oh yeah, for freedom.

Freedom for the rich to feed off the poor. Freedom for criminals and scum to hurt people and get away with it and not have to answer to anyone.

Freedom to get pissed and shove a plant extract up your nose because everyone else does it, and that makes it OK.

Freedom to eat junk and fat and sugar and then complain when you can't breathe and your heart gives out. But it's OK you have the freedom to claim money you don't deserve; other people will pay for the operation to restrict your stomach so you physically can't eat yourself to death.

Oh yes, we have freedom. As long as you agree with the men in suits who carry little red boxes, as long as you think what they tell you to, you can have your freedom.

As long as you work until you can't any more, for no pension and end up dying alone in some God-forsaken hole in your own piss and shit, because the people getting paid minimum wage to look after you haven't got the education to care.

Oh yes, the freedom we enjoy in this country is worth all the life lost. Oh yes.

And the irony is I believed in it once. I believed what I was doing was right, that one man could make a difference.

The truth is this world is far too fucked up. Too evil, too dark for one man to be anything but a speck of dust on the wind.

And in the end none of it matters. We are all heading for the same place.

Gonna go now and get hammered.

Dear Diary,

I can't stand this anymore. I don't want to feel this way any more. I can't stand the nightmares any more. I can't stand the flashbacks; one minute I'm here the next I'm back there.

Not even the drink numbs the pain any more. I want it to end. I want it to all go away.

I don't know what to do.

Dear Diary,

I've found a way out. I was looking for a DVD in my room and I found a noose. The one my Mum threw at me when she was depressed.

It's too small for me but I can make another.

I need time to think. Time to plan. How am I going to do this?

DECEMBER

Dear Diary,

I haven't written for ages because I have been busy. I'm nearly ready now. Let me tell you what I'm going to do.

On the 15 of December I am going to hang myself.

I am going to get dressed in my number twos, the same uniform I wore when I became a soldier, the same uniform I wore when I got my medals. It's only right that I should wear it on the day I die.

I've done all the calculations. I worked out how big a drop I would need to snap my neck. I might be wrong, but it doesn't matter, it will only take a few minutes for me to choke.

I went to B&Q and bought some rope that would hold my weight.

I'm going to do it in the front room. I drilled a hole in the beams. I always thought they were for decoration, turns out they support the ceiling.

I've even picked a song to do it to. *Vale Decem* from *Doctor Who*. That's the music that the tenth Doctor regenerates into the eleventh on the Christmas special. It's awesome.

And then when it gets to the crescendo, right before the fanfare, I'm going to jump.

Wonder if I will regenerate. Hopefully not.

The 15th will be when my Mum is in Blackpool with the darts team. I'll have the house to myself.

Anyway, gonna go, got some stuff to sort out.

Dear Diary,

I'm almost ready. Not long now. I've got my affairs in order as it were. I'm going to send this to *Combat Stress*. Let them have the shrinks take a look. There'll probably have a field day. You never know they might even get someone to turn it into a book and publish it.

Anyway, I have wrote letters to my Mum and Dad. And one to Shell.

In my Mum and Dad's I just said all the things I could never say to them face to face. I put:

Dear Mum and Dad,

If you are reading this, then I'm dead. I'm sorry I couldn't be the son you wanted me to be. I'm sorry for all the pain I put you through. I always wanted to be a soldier. I'm sorry.

But I would like to thank you both for everything you have done for me over the years. You were always there when I needed you and you were the best Mum and Dad anyone could hope to get. Thank you for all the happy memories of growing up: you are both good parents. It's not your fault. I was just too weak, I wasn't strong enough. I'm sorry I didn't become a man you could both be proud of.

Please do not be upset. I think it would be better if you thought that I had died over there and in a way I did. Just know that I love you both very much and hope you have all the good things in life that you deserve.
Goodbye.

Your loving son,
Tommy.

I thought of writing one for each of them but then they both brought me up, so I just did one.

Then I wrote one to Shell. I don't know why, I just felt like I needed to explain to her. I put:

Dear Shell,

This will be the last letter I ever send you. By the time you read this I will be dead.

I just want to say that I will always love you and I am sorry. I'm sorry for all the things I did to you. I'm sorry that the man you fell in love with went away. I'm sorry I couldn't be that man. You were the most special person I ever knew.

I want to thank you for loving me once. I know you have moved on, but you loved me once. I am so grateful that I had you in my life for the time that I did, and I hope that you get all that you hope for in life. I hope that you have children with a man that you deserve. I hope you lead a long and happy life, My Michelle.

Just know that I never stopped loving you, I just didn't have the strength to make you understand. Do you remember when I told you about the stars? That wherever I was in the world, all you had to do was look up, and I would be looking up at the exact same stars that you were, and we would be together; all you had to do was look at the stars and I would be with you.

Well, I want you know that whenever you're scared or feeling down and you have had enough, well, just look up at the stars and I will be with you.

Yours forever,

Tommy.

And then there's this diary. When I have written the last entry I am going to put it in an envelope with the address for *Combat Stress* on it.

So that's it, the only thing left to do now is wait.

I have everything I need; I got some parade gloss and Brasso today, everything's ready.

Now all I have to do is wait.

Dear Diary,

This is my last entry. Today is December the 15th.

As I write I'm stood in my front room in my uniform. Everything is ready. I had to put *Vale Decem* on to a CD 'cos we haven't got a docking station.

All morning I have been getting my uniform ready. I have Brassoed my buttons and belt; I have polished my boots so you can see your face in them, just like on parade. I'm ready.

In a minute I'm going to press Play. Then I'm going to step on to the crate, put the noose round my neck. Then, when the music gets to two minutes twenty-one seconds I'm going to step off. And my life will be over.

I don't know what is waiting for me when I die. Something? Nothing? To be honest, I don't really care. I just want to stop the pain of this world. I just want it to stop.

Anyway, thanks, Diary. Thanks for being there. Thanks for listening. To use a famous phrase: It's been emotional.

I don't know what to write now. What are good last words? I don't know.

I'll just keep it simple.

Goodbye.

—

Postscript

Dear Diary,

I'm still alive. I couldn't do it.

I closed the diary. Pressed Play. I stepped on to the crate and put the noose round my neck.

I let the music wash over me; let it build until the crescendo. Then something strange happened.

As I was about to jump, the winter sun hit the window; the light bounced off my medals and hit the mirror, which sent it into my eyes.

It was like having a flashback, but this was different.

People talk about your life flashing before your eyes. I could see Shell smiling at me, I could see my Mum and Dad's faces when I passed out of Basic, the pride they had. I could see Kev and all the times we laughed together. I could see Jamie's face and his eyes light up as he read his comics. I saw the flag. I saw all the people at Wootton Bassett.

Then I saw myself, stood there in my uniform, with a noose round my neck. I had tears streaming from my eyes.

And all I could think was, what the fuck am I doing.

As the music reached the fanfare I took the noose off and got down. I could hardly stand.

I saw the refection in the mirror and felt something I hadn't felt for a long time.

Pride.

And then it hit me. I realised something.

This was wrong. This was not how to go out. This was a coward's way out.

I was a British soldier. We don't do that. We never surrender. And we never give up. That's for other people. I realised that despite all the pain and heartache and suffering that there is in the world, there is good as well.

There is good in this world.

The love of another; the bonds between family, friendship. These are the things that I fought for. These things are still worth fighting for. They are worth staying alive for.

I will love my Mum and Dad whether they are together or not. I just want them both to be happy.

I will meet another girl and fall in love again.

I will always remember the friends I have lost: Kev, Johno, the Sarge, Jamie. I will honour their memory by living, by leading a good life.

I stood in the mirror and looked at my medals. Then I did the bravest thing I have ever done.

I picked up the phone.

I rang *Combat Stress*. I told them about me, about what I was feeling. They talked to me for ages. They told me I wasn't the only one. There were thousands like me, who all felt the same way.

They said they would send someone to come and see me.

I felt like a weight had been lifted. I wasn't alone in this any more.

I don't know what comes next. It will probably mean some hard work; I will have to face my demons.

But I will beat them. Because I was a British soldier. A part of me always will be.

And one thing you can guarantee about British soldiers.

We never, ever, run away from a fight.

END

Author's Note

First things first. I hope you enjoyed the book. In case you are not aware, what you have just read is a work of fiction. Tommy Atkins is not real.

Or is he?

"Tommy Atkins" is the colloquial nickname for all British soldiers, a tradition that first started in World War I.

Some of you may be thinking "of course we knew what a Tommy was". Unfortunately, as I was writing the book, when you get that familiar question all writers get "what's it called?", I found that not a lot of people under 30 knew what the term meant.

The book was written to raise awareness of an issue that affects thousands of serving and former members of the armed forces and their families.

I had/have PTSD, admittedly not as severe as Tommy but the symptoms are the same.

My job here, as writer, was to entertain and engage. If you are reading this then you have finished the book (one presumes), and hopefully I have done my job.

But I have a feeling that Tommy is more real than I first thought.

When I first met the people from Combat Stress, I was shocked: absolutely shocked at the number of people they had on their books.

The suicide rate amongst veterans is disproportionately high, compared with other demographics in our society.

I hope, very much that there will be people out

there who read this and realise they are not alone. That all they have to do is pick up the phone.

On a more personal note, this is my first published work (I hope, the first of many) and I thank you, the reader, for your time.

I would also like to thank Combat Stress for all the magnificent work they do.

We fight your wars, they fight our battles.

And remember PTSD is a normal reaction to an abnormal situation.

Thank you.

Neil Blower.

the future for heroes

REMOUNT

**Providing a handrail for Servicemen
and women on the road to civilian life**

Remount Objectives:

- To provide personnel of the armed forces of all ranks and status and their dependants with the tools, techniques, and procedures for managing the dramatic change in cultures on resuming civilian life and to teach them how to take control of their lives and achieve their full potential

- To establish a centre of excellence for the training of future teachers and executives of the remount programme

- To cooperate with other projects sharing our ideals

For further information visit: **www.remount.net**

Charity No. 1139264

Garrison Girls is on a mission!

We aim to raise £5million to set up a retreat where we can offer treatment and support to Post Traumatic Stress Disorder sufferers and their families.

We will be one of the first places in the UK to do this. Its focus is on supporting Military PTSD sufferers and their families; treating the family as a whole unit.

The retreat will be able to offer a wide range of treatments to help them recover and overcome the trauma they have experienced.

Our objective is to help stop the devastation of PTSD from breaking down a family and help ALL the victims of PTSD.

For more information please visit our website

WWW.GARRISONGIRLS.COM

FireStep
Publishing

FireStep Publishing is a new division of *Tommies Guides Military Booksellers and Publishers*, first establised in 2005 by Ryan Gearing. Our aim is to publish up to 100 books and related product a year and bring new and old titles alive for the military enthusiast whilst having the ability and desire through many of our book projects to work with and to suport HM Forces and related charities.

We offer an unparalleled range of services from traditional publishing through to subsidised self-publishing and bespoke packages for the discerning and specialist author, historian, genealogist, museum or organisation. We are always looking for new ideas and ventures and especially welcome enquiries from military museums and organisations with a view to partnering in publishing projects.

We pride ourselves on our commitment to each book and our authors, our professionalism and being able to work solely within the military genre, with the knowledge, contacts and expertise to maximise the potential of any of our products.

**For more information on any of our titles,
to contact us with suggestions for new books,
or just to keep in touch please visit our website:
www.firesteppublishing.com**

Available now and coming soon...

Shell Shock: the diary of Tommy Atkins
Neil Blower
ISBN 9781908487025

Enduring Freedom: an Afghan Anthology
Commemorating 10 Years in Afghanistan
Ryan Gearing
ISBN 9781908487018

Massacre at Passcendaele: the New Zealand Story (new ed.)
Glyn Harper
ISBN 9781908487032

British Artillery and Ammunition 1914-1918 (new ed.)
Ian Hogg & Les Thurston
ISBN 9781908487124

London. Bombed, Blitzed and Blown Up
Ian Jones, MBE
ISBN 9781908487148

Whizzbangs and Woodbines
Tales of work and play on the Western Front
Rev. J.C.V. Durrell
ISBN 9781908487100

FireStep
Publishing

**For more information on any of our titles,
to contact us with suggestions for new books,
or just to keep in touch please visit our website:
www.firesteppublishing.com**